Copyright © [2022] by [Bex Dawn] All rights reserved. No portion of this book may be reproduced in any form without written permission from the publisher or author, except as permitted by U.S. copyright law. All rights reserved. No part of this publication may be reproduced, stored or transmitted in any form or by any means, electronic, mechanical, photocopying, recording, scanning, or otherwise without written permission from the publisher. It is illegal to copy this book, post it to a website, or distribute it by any other means without permission. This novel is entirely a work of fiction. The names, characters and incidents portrayed in it are the work of the author's imagination. Any resemblance to actual persons, living or dead, events or localities is entirely coincidental.

Bex Dawn asserts the moral right to be identified as the author of this work. Bex Dawn has no responsibility for the persistence or accuracy of URLs for external or third-party Internet Websites referred to in this publication and does not guarantee that any content on such Websites is, or will remain, accurate or appropriate. Designations used by companies to distinguish their products are often claimed as trademarks. All brand names and product names used in this book and on its cover are trade names, service marks, trademarks and registered trademarks of their respective owners. The publishers and the book are not associated with any product or vendor mentioned in this book. None of the companies referenced within the book have endorsed the book.

Cover Photo Credit: Adobe Stock

PA/Proofread: Bound To Please PA Services

Santa's coming to town,
and he wants a very white Christmas.

# Trigger Warnings

Proceed with caution and remember to practice self-care before, during, and after reading this series. Enjoy!

Things you'll find in this sweet/spicy book:

Age-Gap (big)

Low to No Angst- This is a SWEET and spicy holiday novella

Instalove/instalust

OTT-possessive hero

Healing heart heroine who is pregnant as a result of an assault and her journey to happiness

Spicy book with talk about babies/pregnancy/breeding

Pregnancy kink

A taste of Lactation Kink *Please be aware. This is lactation as a kink. NOT adult breastfeeding. It's primal, filthy, and milky. Kinda sweet, mostly kinky*

Stuffing/stretching

Filling/Swaddling

Current pregnancy

If you have a specific trigger and are unsure if it's in this book or one of my others, please do not hesitate to reach out and ask. The best way is through email or Instagram.

# A Note

As is with the entire Carnal Expectations Series, this Novella celebrates the partners who will go above and beyond for the person they love. Logan read Shiloh's Kindle and literally took notes before buying *tools* that he didn't quite possess on his own, just to make her fantasies come true. Wolfe created a whole-ass alter-ego to figure out what Rayvn enjoyed and then went out of his way to become those things for her. Nicolai Saint is no different. The way he bends for Tinsley is everything. He reads the baby books. Makes the doctor calls. Studies the baby-safe positions. Point is...he's top tier hubby material.

In this novella, we get to see Tinsley find the HEA she so badly deserves. We also get a taste of some interesting kinks.

The lactation kink in this book was inspired by a conversation I had with a dear friend of mine who simply asked...

"Why isn't leaking *during* pregnancy talked about and normalized more?"

Well, lover. Now it is.

# SANTA'S BABY

## CARNAL EXPECTATIONS

# BEX DAWN

# Chapter One

## November 15th

## TINSLEY SNOW

R<sup>UN.</sup> Run.

Run.

That's all my life has ever been. Running. Running from my mind. Running from my past. Running from the memories.

*Running from my goddamned self.*

I thought I'd finally found peace. Happiness. A future. I thought I'd finally found my place in this world. Then...*he* happened.

I place my hand on my belly, rub the painful spot beneath my ribs, and smile.

And then....*she happened.*

Well, I think she's a she. I haven't confirmed the gender yet. Haven't given my baby a name or planned for our future. Hell, I haven't even created a safe place for her to go when she comes into this world. How can I plan for the future when my present is so unstable? So terrifying.

Planning for the future is impossible when you're barely surviving the present.

Sighing, I shake away the morose thoughts and wipe away the tears I didn't even realize I'd cried. I try so hard to be strong. Not just for me but for her. I may not have my shit together, but I will.

*I will.*

"I promise, Pixie," I murmur, using the nickname I've found myself partial to while soothing the aching place where her elbow's lodged. She spins and flips, feeling more like a blue whale than the tiny magical creature that used to flutter around in my belly.

Now that I'm 34 weeks pregnant, her movements have become more uncomfortable than anything. It doesn't help that I'm naturally quite small. I swear, there is absolutely nowhere else for this baby to go. She's out of room, and if I didn't know any better, I'd say my ribs are seconds from snapping. She gives a kick as if to prove my point that she is, in fact, cramped for space.

"We still have over a month to go," I groan, pulling the lever to incline my seat. "Please stop growing so fast and digging into mommy's organs."

She pulls her foot back and settles down, ever the obedient baby. I smile, wiping away another stray tear. I don't know where I'd be without her. What started off as the worst experience of my life, which is saying a lot considering the way I was raised, has quickly become the best thing that's ever happened to me. At a time when I should have felt utterly and heartbreakingly alone, she's been my rock. We're a team. And we will be for the rest of our lives.

"It's just you and me, Little Pix." She obviously doesn't respond, but a sudden warmth that has nothing to do with the heat pipping in from my car vents washes over me as if to soothe. She gets it. We'll be okay.

My stomach lets out a loud, painful growl, and I swallow thickly, my eyes darting across the vacant, snowy mall parking lot. I grab the thick stack of blankets piled on top of me and toss them into the back seat for later. I glance down at the small pile of bags on the passenger floorboard to make sure everything's still safely stowed away. Finding my belongings and windows intact, I exhale a shaking breath. We made it through another night.

Bending over the center console takes more work now that my belly is so huge, but I quickly dig out my nearly empty purse from beneath the pile. Dropping it onto my lap, I roll my shoulders back, fighting the urge to cry again. It's the hormones, I swear. It has absolutely nothing to do with the fact that I *know* what's inside my purse, even without looking. It's not much. Not anymore. But it's enough to keep us both fed and our temporary home filled with gas until I find us a safe place to settle down. It has to be. Then...

Then, I'll give her everything she deserves and more. A home. A warm bed. A fully stocked fridge. A happy, *safe* place to exist.

But first, food.

Like ripping off a band-aid, I tug my wallet out and look through the various bills and spare change. Counting and counting again as if that will magically make the meager contents multiply.

It won't, but hell...even 21-year-olds can wish for a Christmas miracle.

"$162.39," I breathe. "Looks like all-you-can-eat pancakes again." I shove the money back into my wallet with more force than necessary and toss my purse onto the passenger seat. My eyes flick down to the gas gauge, finding half a tank left. Enough to get me where I need to go and keep the heater running. My lip tips up. Santa may not be granting me any Christmas wishes this year, but I can still be thankful for the tiny miracles surrounding me.

The drive to the diner I've frequented these last few weeks is relatively quick, considering the mall parking lot I've been sleeping in is smack dab in the center of town. I crank the heater up and then the music after tuning into the local station. It's a Christmas song—as usual. I grin, butterflies filling my chest. I love Christmas. I always have. Maybe my love for the holiday is what drew me to this adorable town in the first place.

Jackson, Wyoming.

It's a far cry from the tiny country town I grew up in, Blue River, Colorado. All and all, Blue River is a sweet, charming place filled with wonderful people and miles of mountain terrain. It's beautiful, quiet, and relatively sleepy. But it's also close-knit and small, which, for someone like me, is annoying. No. It's worse than that. It's downright *damaging*. I couldn't handle the constant stream of gossip that surrounded me. It's not new. Blue River is full of gossips that are borderline bullies when they catch on to a juicy story, and for me, that's basically my entire life.

Born on the wrong side of the tracks. The poor, scrawny girl in the shitty trailer park that hasn't seen a day of maintenance since it was created. The one who always looked far too small for her own age due to a short height and a steady lack of food. The one with the torn and stained clothing that never fit in. The girl with the abusive, alcoholic father. The one whose mom abandoned her at the hospital the day she was born, leaving her with that crappy father. A father who never wanted her and made that known *again and again and again*—

I never gave up, though. I fought tooth and nail to get out of that trailer park. I stuck to my schoolwork. Graduated. Worked odd jobs every chance I got just to save up enough money to move out the second I was able.

And I did.

I moved two hours away to Denver. Found a tiny little studio apartment above a laundromat. A cat named Stella. A job at a convenience store that was willing to work with my hours, enabling me to attend a business course at the adult school in town. It took me almost a year to receive my certificate, allowing me the opportunity to seek better employment. I sent out hundreds of applications and resumes, expecting the worst but hoping for the best.

Denial after denial met my attempts. Until finally, it didn't. I was unbelievably happy. I was also young and naïve. Too naïve to see that the job I landed was way too good to be true. Too young to know any better. Too quiet to speak up when I should have. And too terrified to do anything about it.

And then—it was too late.

At the age of twenty, I was offered a position as the secretary to Colorado's Chief of Police, Vincent Sutton. He was kind, funny, and at the age of 56, much older than me. I trusted him. I shouldn't have. Like I said...naïve.

One night, he asked me to stay late and help with filing some paperwork. I was eager for overtime and an increase in my responsibilities. I gladly accepted. It took less than an hour after everyone had left for him to make his move. There, in his official office, with his accolades and awards surrounding us, he stole something from me that was not freely offered.

It was brutal. Painful. Soul destroying.

He then threatened to arrest me if I told anyone. He threatened to send me to worse places than the trailer park I grew up in. He threatened to take the tiny ounce of safety and home I'd found in those two years since leaving my father's clutches. Clutches I'd only just escaped.

He scared me into submission, and then he convinced me that I'd wanted it. Asked for it. That no one would believe someone like me over someone like him.

So, I did *nothing*. I said *nothing*.

I continued to do my job, but all the while, I was breaking inside. Shattering irreparably. Until a chance encounter with another woman changed everything. Georgia Kingsley, Sutton's previous secretary and rape victim.

At the time of her attack, she'd been brave enough to do what I hadn't. She'd gone to the hospital. DNA was taken. Police reports were made. But nothing came of it. Why would it when you're going up against the man who rules over the entire state? We knew it was a losing battle. We knew we stood no chance, yet, we had to try. We chose to go to another police station a few towns over. File reports and hope for the best.

The best came, and her name was Rayvn Porter. An attorney who took our case pro-bono. Sutton was arrested. Trials were had. Unfortunately, even Ray, a woman whom I now call my friend, was no match for Vincent Sutton and the power he wields. Not only is he the Police Chief, but so were his father and grandfather. He comes from old money and practically owns all of Colorado. He has every judge, cop, and evidence tech in his pocket.

It was a losing battle.

One that Georgia couldn't handle and walked away from months in. One that I tried to fight. Tried with all I had to power through. To win. But—when Sutton demanded I get an amniocentesis while only twenty weeks pregnant, despite my doctor's warnings against it, I too chose to walk away.

In the choice between my baby and justice for myself—I chose her.

And I would, again and again. I will. Always. She is my priority. She has been from the moment that stick turned blue and will be until the day I die. I refuse to allow her to have the same kind of life I've had. One full of fear, bruises, and hunger. One where a man rules her life. Her dreams. Her security. *Fuck that.* So, if that means I live out of my car and run for my life until I find a safe place for us to settle down, so be it.

Day by day. That's all I can do. Take it day by day.

I blink back the burning in my eyes and focus on the world around me instead of my depressing thoughts and the ugly memories that inevitably come with them.

This town is hands down one of the cutest places I've ever seen. It may be a little over a week from Thanksgiving, but Jackson clearly has an obsession with Christmas. The streets are white and snowy from the continual soft fall of flakes. The white string lights hung from the lamp posts, crisscrossing over the road, making it look like some sort of winter wonderland. Downtown is full of old shops decorated for the upcoming holiday. Christmas trees and bright colors fill every window with beautiful displays. People mill about, laughing and swinging heavy shopping bags back and forth. Kids bundled in their warmest clothes skip with their parents. Steam billows from a coffee cart. A woman walking a tiny French bulldog wearing a buffalo check sweater laughs as she runs across the street to catch up with friends.

It's literally adorable. There is no other word to describe it. I feel as though I've fallen into an alternate universe or maybe a Hallmark special. I slow to a stop at a four-way crossing, and my burning eyes almost turn to an ugly sob when an elderly couple smiles and waves at me as though we're old friends. I've driven from town to town. Across state lines. Through farmlands and big cities. I've been on the run. Constantly moving from place to place *for months*. Yet, this is the first town I've wanted to stay in. This is the first place that has screamed for me to plant roots. To settle down. To find a way to make it work.

It's going to *kill me* to leave tomorrow. But I have no choice. I've already stayed too long. Now that the trials have been dropped, Sutton is a free man. He should be moving on. He should be leaving Georgia and me to ourselves to pick up the pieces and start over with our lives. He should...*but he's not.*

I shoot a scowl over to my dead cell phone. There had been no new messages when I checked it a few days ago, but I can't help the pang of anxiety that fills me every time it goes off. Maybe that's why I let the battery die all the time. I could find a place to charge it, or hell, even invest in a car charger, but I enjoy the silence I find when I have no connection to the outside world. To him. Unfortunately, I have a phone call to make so I'll have to charge it at the diner. A lump forms in my throat at the thought.

*Will today be the day I get another threatening message? Will today be the day he makes good on his promise to take it all away?*

My mind flits over the last few texts I received since this all began, and nausea climbs up my throat, making a home next to the ball of emotions living there.

**Unknown: You'll pay for all this bad press, you lying bitch.**

**Unknown: I'm going to take everything from you like you've been trying to do to me.**

**Unknown: I should never have let you get away.**

**Unknown: Open your mouth again, and you're dead.**

**Unknown: That's not my kid. Stop lying, slut.**

I know without a shadow of a doubt that they're from him. *Sutton.* No one else would threaten me like that. The way he did that day in his office. No one. At first, I ignored the messages. He was in jail, and I knew he couldn't hurt me. But then, the case was dropped, and he was set free. The messages increased in frequency and intensity. The last ones being the worst.

**Unknown: I'm coming for you. I won't let you fuck up my life anymore.**

**Unknown: It's funny that you think you can run from me.**

**Unknown: You're dead.**

**Unknown: Chasing you has been fun, but I'm done playing.**

I pull into the parking lot of the cute diner and park my car. A shudder works its way down my spine as I think of the last message he sent me. The one that finally forced me to cross state lines, leaving Colorado once and for all.

**Unknown: I'm going to enjoy killing that bastard inside of you while you still breathe, bitch.**

That was three weeks ago, the day before Halloween. I haven't heard from him since, but my gut refuses to allow me to fall into a false sense of security over his silence. He's out there. He has to be. And until he's found or dies, I won't be safe. Neither of us will.

I roll my shoulders and reach over my console to snag my heavy jacket and purse, pushing the thoughts and emotions away. I have a baby to feed, and I refuse to allow Vincent Sutton to keep me from ensuring she's healthy. I may not be able to give her everything yet, but I can do this.

*Day by day by, day.*

# Chapter Two

## TINSLEY SNOW

LOOKING IN THE REARVIEW mirror, I groan when I take in the state of myself. My snow-white skin is pink and splotchy from crying. My long pale blonde hair that lands just above my butt is in a greasy bun that's disheveled from sleep. My ice-blue eyes stand out even more than normal, thanks to the dark bags beneath them. My cheeks are swollen, and at this point, I'm not sure whether that's from pregnancy or the never-ending tears I've cried over the last year. Either way,

I look every bit as exhausted and worn down as I am.

"I need a vacation from life," I murmur, doing my best to make myself presentable. A piece of my gross hair slips from my messy topknot, refusing to stay in place. I grimace. "And a shower."

The money I've been using since I left Denver two months ago is almost completely gone after staying at hotels in the various towns I've been to. The nest egg I'd managed to save for myself wasn't huge by any means but had I been able to continue working and living in my cheap studio; it would have lasted. Hell, it would have probably doubled by now.

Pain slices through me. I'm not sure how much longer I can do this. A week, maybe two, at most before I'll have to find a safe place to settle down. I can't be on the run with a newborn. More than that, I can't live in my car with her. I refuse to not give my child everything she deserves. And it's so much more than I ever had.

Content with my appearance, I slide out of my car, my back popping and aching as I stand. I quickly wrap myself up in my coat before trudging through the snow toward the diner. *The Frosty Spoon* is old and charming but clearly well-loved. The staff is sweet. The food is excellent. But, more importantly—*The Frosty Spoon* is warm and cheap.

The overhead bell dings as I step inside. The air from the heater hits my freezing face. I grit my teeth, feeling like tiny knives are pricking at my skin. My cold, wet feet burn, reminding me once more that I need new boots stat. I scrunch my toes up and away from the holes in the split seams, hoping to bring some life back to them. My stomach growls again, this time louder. I shoot a silent thank you to whoever is listening that the diner is busy, and the loud hum of chatter and Christmas music drowns out the embarrassing sound.

"Mornin', Darlin'," Lottie, the curvy, sweet shop owner that I've come to adore, greets. I smile widely and shoot her a somewhat awkward wave, my fingers tucked deeply in the sleeve of my coat. She chuckles and jerks her chin toward an empty two-seater in the far corner. "Get on over there and cozy up. I'll bring you some coffee."

"Decaf," I call out to her retreating form. She shoots me a wink over her shoulder, her eyes trailing down my body and zeroing in on my huge belly. Her smile wavers, a look of concern filling her ruddy cheeks. I swallow, shrugging off what looks to be a good amount of pity.

I hate it, but it's better than the disgusted looks I'd receive if I was still living in Blue River. Don't get me wrong; it's a nice town with good people. But my ex-boss, aka the man who raped me, is fucking *worshipped* there. Not only is he the Chief of Police, but he was recently promoted to Police Commissioner. Because, of course, he was. Men of power and wealth can do no wrong. A little assault trial clearly did nothing to dampen his public image. As soon as Georgia and I had chosen to go up against him, the townspeople started throwing hate our way. Just as Sutton always taunted…

Who would believe two girls from the slums against a man with all the money, power, and influence in the world? No one, that's who.

I groan, rolling my eyes. I don't hate many people, but I do hate him, and all of the other men out there like him. Self-entitled, rich, chauvinistic pigs who don't understand the meaning of *no*.

"Pricks," I mutter, sliding out of my jacket and tossing it aside before slowly dropping into my seat. "All of them."

The old man sitting at the table next to me shoots me an odd look, and I barely stifle a wince. I smile softly, thankful I didn't mutter the *who* I was referring to when I stupidly spoke out loud. He laughs quietly and tips his coffee back.

"We are, honey. The lot of us. And don't you ever forget it." A blush breaks out on my face, mortal embarrassment and humor warring for dominance in my chest.

See—this is why I love this town so much. People are just...*normal*. Kind, light-hearted, good-natured, and normal. Also observant, apparently.

"Here you go," Lottie chirps, sliding a massive cup of decaf in front of me, already decked out with the white chocolate peppermint creamer I love so much and a hefty dollop of whipped cream. She even went the extra mile and sprinkled peppermint flakes across the top, making it the perfect Christmas pick-me-up.

It takes both of my hands to lift the steaming cup. My eyes drift shut as I take my first sip. The flavors explode across my tongue, and my little one does a happy flip in my belly at the warm liquid. I let out a happy sigh and blink up at Lottie, smiling in thanks. Her blonde ponytail bobs to the side as she tilts her head, observing me.

"How you doin', Darlin'? And don't lie to me. You know I see right through it." I groan, some of the cheer I'd felt from the drink fizzling out.

One of the busboys passes by, sliding a glass of water next to my coffee and grinning down at me. A small zing of appreciation travels straight down to my clit at the sight of it. I swear, if I'm not crying, I'm horny. Pregnancy hormones are wack. Besides, he's super cute. My age, probably, or a little younger. That's not normally my type. I like older men. What can I say...*daddy issues*.

The busboy, whose name is Luke, tosses me a wink that, in my old life, would probably have me melting. Unfortunately, that's no longer something that happens to me. Especially not with him. I have nothing against men my age or people who work in restaurants, but after everything I've been through, Luke isn't what I need. I need to stand on my own two feet, and when I do decide to find a man to spend my life with, I refuse to settle for anyone who doesn't have his shit together. It's not just me; Tinsley Snow, the girl from the trailer park, I have to worry about anymore. No. Now I have Pixie. The time for hot jocks, late nights, and leather jackets is officially over.

Lottie snaps, gaining my attention. I grimace, realizing I'd been staring after Luke long after he'd disappeared into the kitchen. He may not be my type, but his ass is phenomenal.

"I'm alright," I murmur, swallowing another sip of coffee to stall. She tuts, tapping her kitten heel on the shiny grey tile floor. I sigh. "I'm cold. Hungry. Broke. And in need of a very hot shower with a bucket of shampoo." I dig my phone from my bag, passing it to her with the charger. "And I need to make a call."

She blinks rapidly, her eyes glossy. She shakes her head and grabs my phone, knowing the drill by now. "You can't keep doing this, Tinsley," she mumbles, disapproval thick in her voice. "If you just decided to stay, we could find you—"

"You know I can't, Lottie," I whisper, my hands flexing around the mug. She may not know everything that happened, but she knows enough. Enough to realize that her argument about me settling down in Jackson is useless.

It takes her a moment to pull herself together, words clearly sitting on her tongue. Finally, she nods once. "All-you-can-eat pancakes are still on the menu for another two hours." Her eyes flit down to my belly again. "But that baby girl needs protein. Not just carbs. I'm bringin' you eggs." She turns away from me, still rambling as she goes. "And sausage. Maybe I'll get Oscar to fry you up some hash. Oh. I'll chop up some fruit. Need lots of folic acid at this stage."

I chuckle, knowing that just as useless as Lottie's argument for me to stay here is, my trying to dissuade her from overfeeding me is a waste of breath. Lottie and her husband, Oscar, own *The Frosty Spoon,* and she's constantly telling me that it's her business to do with as her heart desires. Apparently, her heart desires to make me gain twenty pounds every time I come in.

I've barely finished my cup of steaming decaf, my body officially defrosted, when the first plate of food is delivered. I say first because Oscar's idea of all-you-can-eat pancakes means a massive overflowing stack that he happily replenishes the second you dig you. Minutes later, the eggs, sausage, hash, and potatoes Lottie insisted I eat arrive. I gape at the spread, unsure what the heck I'm supposed to do with all of it.

My huge eyes snap up to meet hers. Unsurprisingly, she's smiling and nodding at the feast with pride. "Lottie," I murmur, setting my fork down gently, my throat burning. "This is enough food to feed an army. It's too much." I say that not only because it's a shit ton of food but because I know there is no way she's going to let me pay for it. She never does.

The second time I came in here, I figured out that my $7.00 bill was worth well over $40. I tried to pay her. She refused to take my money, so I tucked the bills under a used plate and ran out. The next time I came in, she stuffed them into my jacket pocket when I wasn't looking and sent me away with four takeout boxes of extras. It's useless, but still—

She tuts me, crossing her arms over her large breasts. "Do you love your child, Tinsley?"

*Oh, Christ, on a cracker. She's pulling out the big guns.*

"Of course I do," I groan, my hands rubbing the swell of my stomach. Pixie flips in acknowledgment. Or maybe she's just content with the warmth and food surrounding us. "That's not the point."

She huffs, shaking her head. "Yes, it most definitely is. You love that baby, and that baby needs her mama to be healthy and looked after." Lottie's eyes wilt, a look of sadness joining the gang-up-on-Tinsley party. She settles a soft hand on my shoulder and squeezes. "Sometimes, we all need a little help, Sugar. No point in being ashamed to ask for it. Does no one any good. Especially not that baby of yours."

I swallow, my fists clenching so hard my short nails prick into my palms. "It's not a problem of pride, Lott. I know I need help." I shake my head, looking down at my belly.

Okay, maybe it is partially pride. But, more than that, it's just that *I can't*. I can't ask for help here or try to make friends or settle down. I can't because this place will never be my home. Not while *he's* still out there.

Lottie crouches down, grimacing when her knees pop. She tilts my chin up, bringing us eye to eye. This close, I can see the finer lines around her brown eyes that I'd missed before, peeking out from beneath her heavy makeup. Her blonde hair has thick streaks of grey throughout. I don't know how old she is. I've assumed maybe in her early forties. Now, up close, I think it may be closer to fifty, but she's beautiful nonetheless, and her heart truly is pure gold.

"Did I ever tell you I have a daughter?" she asks softly. I tug my lower lip between my teeth and shake my head, turning to face her fully. A wistful look fills her eyes. "I was 19 when I got pregnant with Lily. Her conception wasn't a pretty story, either."

Lottie pauses when I suck in a sharp breath. She nods once as if to confirm my silent question, and I feel myself tearing up for the twentieth time today. I blink back the wetness, refusing to make this about me.

"Yep," she murmurs, clicking her tongue. "My parents kicked me out when I told them I was pregnant. They didn't care how she came to be, just that I didn't have a man and was refusing to give her up."

"I'm so sorry, Lottie," I whisper, squeezing her hand that's now resting on my knee.

She shrugs. "I'm not gonna lie and say life was easy. It wasn't. I moved out. Ran far from home, not wanting to ever see my kid's dad again. Ended up in a shelter for a while. They helped me get on my own feet. Found me a job waitressing. I had no experience, but the owner was a really nice man who saw that I needed a helping hand and gave it to me. Without him, I don't know where I'd be."

I smile, happy that she found her way. Lottie continues before I can say anything.

"What I'm sayin' is that it's okay to get help." She leans in, lowering her voice. "It's also okay to stop runnin' and trust others to keep you safe when the world feels too big and scary to do it alone."

I squeeze my eyes shut, her words hitting their intended target like a bullet. God, how badly I want that. To trust people again. To feel at home. Comfortable. *Safe.*

We sit in silence for a moment, my brain clawing at me to find a new topic of conversation. I open my eyes, her story sinking in fully. Suddenly, I want to know more about this woman whose life sounds so similar to mine. "Whatever happened to that man? Did you keep working for him once you got on your feet?"

She grins, her eyes twinkling in the bright morning light. She cocks a brow and looks over my shoulder. I follow her gaze, finding her staring directly through the small window that looks into the kitchen where a very jolly Oscar is flipping pancakes. My eyes snap back to hers, my cheeks pulsing from how wide my grin is.

"Oscar?" I breathe.

"Yep," she confirms, popping the p as she pushes to stand. Her knees crack again, but she squeezes her hip and groans. "Lookin' at me now, you'd never know the man has twenty years on me." She cackles, her hair dancing back and forth. "Seems I'm not the only one who was called to Jackson, Wyoming, looking for a Christmas miracle." Her brows bob as she gives me a knowing look before disappearing into the kitchen once more.

I watch with fascination as she waltzes up to a very grey but still joyful-looking Oscar and plants a huge kiss on his cheek. She laughs at his surprise

and darts away. He quickly grips her by her thick hips and tugs her backward, pressing her against the counter. I feel like I should look away. Like I'm intruding on a private moment, but I just can't. My gaze stays riveted on the way Oscar stares down at Lottie. His eyes are heated, but his expression is soft. Adoring. Obsessed.
*In love.*
My heart squeezes painfully, and Pixie swishes in my tummy. I love her. More than anything, I love my daughter. But I can't deny the way my soul craves *that.* All consuming, deep, honest-to-God love. I want a man to look at me that way. My hands cradle my stomach, my chest pounding. It would be so nice not to have to do this alone. To be loved, cherished, and protected. But I refuse to settle for anyone who doesn't love my daughter equally. Who doesn't embrace her as though she's his own. Who looks down on how she came to be the way Lottie's parents did. Until I find that in a man, a partner, it's just her and I.

A loud bang followed by a shout has me jumping in my seat, my heart racing on instinct. My head swivels toward the sound, finding a group of people standing out front gaping up at *The Frosty Spoon's* roof. Oscar flies through the kitchen's swinging door with far more speed and grace than a man his age should possess. His panicked eyes follow mine and the rest of the diners, who have all paused their meal to see what the fuss is about.

Another thud.

Then a clang.

A shout.

A gasp.

A heavy pile of snow falls from the roof, followed by the gutter, clattering to the sidewalk. Seconds later, a giant Santa figurine joins the chaos, sled, and all, toppling from the roof. My eyes are huge as they dart back and forth between everything. The mess, the crowd, the diners, and Oscar, who is standing stock-still in the middle of the restaurant, his hands on his hips.

"Well, shit," he mutters, shaking his head. "Lottie," he calls out, sounding exhausted. His eyes remain fixed on the crowd outside that is now trying to sort out the damage. "Santa's down again. Took the gutter with em' this time."

"Bastard," she groans, her voice so close I startle again. My head snaps to my left, finding her standing right next to me. Crap. This is giving me whiplash. She slides my phone and charger onto the table, smiling down at me softly. "No new messages, Darlin'. Make your call."

I release a breath I hadn't realized I'd been holding and nod but can't stop myself from being distracted by their situation.

"Anything I can do to help?" I ask, my gaze flicking back to the windows. I chuckle as I watch three small kids dance around the massive plastic Santa who looks slightly worse for the wear. Oscar and another man are moving the large, cracked rain gutter while a teenage boy shovels the large pile of fallen snow that's blocking the front door. My laughter dies, and a sharp stab of longing hits my chest. This really is a good town filled with good people.

"No," Lottie sighs, pulling out her cell phone. "I'll call Mr. Saint. He'll take care of it."

Ah. Mr. Saint. The man I keep hearing about but have yet to see. Apparently, he's a big deal in this town, but not in the same way as Sutton. He owns the largest toy store chain in the mid-west, *Wonderland*, but calls Jackson his home. I'm not sure how or why, but he's revered in these parts. At this point, I'm beginning to think he's some sort of magical fairy godmother, the way they all speak of him.

"Why would you call Mr. Saint?" I ask, confused as hell. "Does he own the building or something?"

Lottie looks down at me, her fingers pausing on the screen of her phone as she types. Her brow cocks in time with her lip. "Nope. He's just a good man."

My nose scrunches, but before I can ask her to expand on that odd statement, her phone rings. Lottie grins widely and runs outside to Oscar, the device already glued to her ear. I don't know who she's talking to or what's being said, but she looks happy as she relays the information to Oscar. He smiles in return, looking relieved.

I exhale a long breath, my lungs feeling compressed from eating so much while carrying a bowling ball. "Mommy needs some breathing room, please, Little Pix," I mutter. She kicks me hard enough that I swear she's trying to evacuate her living quarters via my belly button, and I damn near double over. *Jesus.* I may only be 5'3, but my kid has legs meant for a track star. "Stop it. I need air to make this call," I grit out.

I recline back in my chair, attempting to stretch out, and bring up Google to search for a local women's clinic. I need to get in to see someone for my 8-month check-up before I head back out on the road. The web browser opens, my fingers hovering over the search bar, but a local news ad pops up, freezing me in place. My phone slips from my hands, a photo of a man I never wanted to see again staring back at me. My heart slams against my already compressed lungs. My breathing becomes shallow and faint. The room starts to spin, and my eyes blur with unshed tears.

Vaguely, I can hear someone talking to me. I hear their words. Can tell that their tone is concerned, but I don't really *hear* them. I'm too focused on the words in front of me on my tiny little phone screen to process anything else.

**Colorado's Police Commissioner, Vincent Sutton, was found dead in his Tahoe vacation home following the release of a recording where he graphically recounted not only raping multiple women but murdering an underage, pregnant female.**

My mind replays the words again and again, committing them to memory. I can't move. Can barely breathe as I try to understand the news.

*It can't be real. Can it? He's dead? Gone for good? No. I refuse to believe it. I refuse to allow myself that hope, that relief. Wait. He murdered someone? Holy shit. I can't be—*

Warm, soft hands on my cheeks bring me back to the present and freeze my spiraling thoughts in their tracks. My eyes are blurry and unseeing until finally, Lottie's face comes into focus.

She's concerned and scared, but—she's here. *I'm not alone.* Oscar, Harriet, and Luke are not far behind her, worry etched across their features. They don't even know me, yet they paused what they were doing because they were worried...*for me.*

I'm not sure anyone's ever cared about me that much, especially a stranger.

I swallow, knowing I need to say something. Knowing I need to tell her what's happened. I open my mouth, but only a choked sob comes out. Her face pales, eyes darting down to my belly.

"Is it the baby? Do we need an ambulance?" she asks, her voice wavering.

I shake my head. My limp arm reaches out blindly, finding my phone. I swallow again, fighting to urge to ugly cry or maybe puke. I pass the phone to Lottie, pressing it against her chest until she's forced to release my face. She exhales a breath and grabs it, her eyes rapidly gliding across the article that I've yet to read fully. Understanding washes over her features, her eyes hardening. She hands my phone back and gives me a look.

"This him?" I nod—no other words needed. A heavy, weighted silence falls between us. It's long and painful, but then, she's smiling. Smiling so massively that I can't help but follow her lead. She bends down again, getting right up in my face, and squeezes my cheeks roughly before wiping away my tears. "You ready to plant them roots, Darlin'?"

A ragged breath wooshes out of me, my voice cracking as I speak. "I think I need a job, Lottie."

# Chapter Three

## TINSLEY SNOW

*THE FROSTY SPOON* WAS, in fact, not hiring. Lottie and Oscar offered to create a position for me, but it would be incredibly minimal hours with little pay. At this point, I'd be happy to take anything, but Lottie insisted I try a few other places in town before settling. So, here I stand in the middle of the biggest toy store I've ever seen in my life, *Wonderland*. Also known as the greatest toy emporium in America.

From what I know, *Wonderland* has been around for over ten years. They're spread out across the mid-west and can be found in malls and large shopping centers all over the place. The company is owned by a man named Nicolai Saint—the same Mr. Saint that Lottie and the rest of the town can't stop talking about. With good reason, too, it seems. The stores are famous in these parts, and not just because of their products, but the man behind them. He has a love for charity and a spirit for giving back to the community—or so the woman who greeted me at the door said right before running to the office to find a manager.

I spin in a circle, my hands cradling my heavy belly as I take in the huge store. It's two stories with an escalator right in the center. Toys line every inch of the shelves that span from the ground up to the second-floor ceiling. Tables covered in imaginative displays pull your eyes from one thing to the next. The sounds of trains, talking toys, nursery rhymes, and children's laughter can barely be heard over the Christmas music playing overhead.

But...that's not what has me grinning ear to ear.

No. It's everything else. If the décor inside of his toy store is anything to go by, Mr. Saint loves Christmas as much as everyone else in Jackson.

What I assume are real pine trees judging by the heavenly smell surrounding me, fill the open spaces between sales displays. Each and every one is decorated with a different theme ranging from dinosaurs to planes, to pink glitter ballerinas, and so on, all with kids in mind. Garland is wrapped around the checkout counter, with red tinsel sprinkled over top. Paper snowflakes hang from the high ceilings, reminding me of the movie Elf.

Actually…the entire store reminds me of that film. Down to the lights, trains, and Lego creations. My brows pinch.

"Holy Buddy the Elf," I murmur with a snort.

A feminine scoff behind me has me jumping and whirling around. I come face to face with an elderly woman not much taller than me, dressed exactly like one of Santa's helpers. Her long-sleeved velvet dress goes down to her knees, showing off candy-cane striped tights and black booties. A thick black belt with a gold buckle cinches her waist, causing the skirt to flare wide. Her short grey bob is partially hidden beneath a matching pointy elf hat, completing the ensemble. She looks completely adorable.

"They stole that idea from us," she snips, placing her delicate wrinkled hands on her hips as she taps a pointed boot. I arch a brow in question, enjoying the fact that I don't have to look up to meet someone's eyes for once. "Those movie people." She waves a flustered hand toward the shop. "They stole that scene from our store. They wouldn't know how to decorate for Christmas if Santa handed them an instruction manual."

My forehead scrunches, still confused. My eyes dart all over the shop, taking in what truly is an uncanny resemblance. "Are you saying the movie people came here and copied *Wonderland* for the film?" I murmur.

She tuts, shaking her head in irritation. "Course they did. *Wonderland's* the first Christmas-themed toy store in the United States. Where else would they have gotten the idea?"

I cock my head to the side, digesting her words. "The store looks like this all year round?" I ask, a hint of shock in my voice that I can't possibly hide. Wow. I wasn't expecting that. "It's not just for the holidays?"

The woman pauses in her silent muttering to stare at me, her pink cheeks drooping. "This your first time in one of our stores?" I nod, rolling back on my heels. Yeah. That's probably not a great thing to admit when trying to get a job. "Hmm," she murmurs, her eyes roaming down my body and taking me in. It makes me immediately uncomfortable as I wait for her judgment over my appearance. Or perhaps about how young I look and the huge belly I'm carrying. The lack of a ring on my wedding finger. Maybe the holes in my shoes or worn jacket. There's a long list to choose from.

It's not new. The judgment. The questions. I'm used to it, but that doesn't mean I'm okay with it. Instead of waiting for her inevitable comment, I begin to fill the awkward silence with a ramble.

"Sorry." I gesture to my belly with a cringe. "I haven't really had time to get out and shop lately." Jesus that sounds bad, especially as I emphasize with a tummy rub. "I just mean, I've had a lot going on, and well, I don't really have enough money to hang out at the mall or spend time in a toy store." She meets my gaze again, both of her bushy grey brows raised. It's unnerving, only making my verbal diarrhea worse. "I definitely should, though. Or will, I mean. With the baby and everything, I'm sure I'll be in toy stores a lot in the future. No. Not toy stores, like plural. Just yours. I'll only shop in your toy story, I swear. I—"

She places her warm hand over my mouth, effectively shutting me up. My lips tuck into my mouth as I gape at her. What did I just say? Holy shit. That was bad. Way to go, Tinsley. You haven't even officially met the woman yet, and you're spilling your words all over her shiny shoes.

"You done?" she quips, not removing her hand.

I nod rapidly, my heart beating uncomfortably in my chest. I feel like I'm going to puke, and that would be terrible. Her lip twitches. Once. Twice. Before she's chuckling loudly. Her hand slides from my face as she continues to shake with laughter at my expense. I exhale a shaky breath, my foot inching backward as I prepare to tuck my tail and run back to *The Frosty Spoon*. I'll take minimum wage and a small workweek over this any day.

Finally, she sighs, wiping her pink cheeks. "That was pretty bad, girly. Really talked yourself into a hole, didn't you?" I groan, palming my face.

"Sorry," I whisper. "I haven't had to apply for a job in—" I break off, swallowing thickly.

I don't want to think about that. Then, I'll start thinking about the last time I worked, and if I do that, I'll think about my old boss. My old boss, who is *dead*, a fact was confirmed by Rayvn before I officially decided to settle down in this perfect town. Nope. Not going there. I shake my head, wetting my dry lips, and meet her gaze once more. All humor has left her face. Surprisingly, it's not pity I find in her brown eyes. Understanding, maybe? That would be impossible. Rolling my shoulders back, I thrust my hand out in offering.

"Hi," I say softly. "My name is Tinsley Snow. I'm new to Jackson and in need of a job. Lottie thought you might be hiring seasonally."

It takes her a moment to respond, but she nods and smiles, placing her hand in mine. "Nice to meet you, Tinsley. I'm Candy Cane, the manager of *Wonderland*." She must see my many, *many* questions over her name because she snickers and shrugs, sliding her hand into a hidden pocket I hadn't noticed before. Love that. "My name is actually Candance, but all of the employees have an elf name. I've just had mine for so long; no one calls me by my real name anymore."

I nod, following her as she turns and beckons me to follow. Candy gives me a tour of the shop, and all the while, she prattles on about the creation of *Wonderland* and the story of its origin. The first girl I'd met here was young, possibly even in High School. She was sweet as she gushed about how incredible working here is and how much she adores Mr. Saint. I swear, she had hearts in her eyes as she spoke of the man. It was surprising, to be honest. After hearing about him for the last few weeks, his accomplishments, success, and money, I assumed he'd be an old man, maybe closer to Candy Cane's age.

After the lengthy and informative tour, I find myself panting and struggling to keep up with her as we enter her office. I've long since removed my jacket and scarf. My body is officially defrosted, and I'm starving, despite eating nearly all of Oscar and Lottie's food a few hours ago. Something my stomach makes known the second I smell the delicious gingerbread candle burning in the large upstairs office. Honestly, it looks more like a small apartment than anything.

There's a big, open room with a desk covered in papers on one side. A small kitchenette sits opposite, complete with a sink, counter, fridge, and microwave. A tiny two-seater table is nestled against the wall. There's a short hallway off to the side, and from here, I can see three doors. The office is decorated as though Santa did a line of peppermint crack and threw up everywhere. It's white, red, and green with candy décor on every surface. While it's not my taste...*at all*...I can definitely see how well it suits Candace.

She notices me gaping at the door and huffs a breath, rolling her eyes. She grabs my hand as though we're old friends instead of manager and potential employee.

"Come with me. We have something to take care of. Then you can rest." I follow along, feeling a little bit like a lost puppy as she leads me down the hall and into another room. It's small but cozy. There's a wall of windows, letting in natural light. A tan couch is pushed up against a wall, covered in Christmas pillows and throw blankets. On the opposite wall is a floor-to-ceiling mirror. Candy guides me to a three-inch platform in front of the mirror, shoving me softly until she has me where she wants me. Silently, she takes my belongings and drops them on the couch before removing my cardigan. I stand there, mouth open, eyes wide as this sweet old woman practically strips me until I'm left in just my thick fleece-lined leggings, long-sleeved t-shirt, and soggy socks. I don't know why I don't speak up or stop her. Maybe because I feel an odd kinship with Candy. She's kind, if not a little sassy. Definitely a lot bossy. She reminds me of the old Tinsley. The one who fought tooth and nail to make something of herself. I'd definitely love to get the version of me back.

*I will*, I tell myself. *I can*. Things are different now. Vincent is dead. I can do anything. *Anything*.

I smile, relief soaring through me so rapidly that I get a little woozy. Candy catches me by my elbow, drawing my attention back from my thoughts. She says nothing, passing me a bottle of water. She cocks a brow, hands on her hips. Never looking away, I drink half the bottle in one go, not realizing how thirsty I was. She nods approvingly, taking the bottle from my hands and swapping it for a pack of peanut butter crackers. My stomach growls again, Pixie making her needs known very loudly.

"Thank you." I smile, digging into the snack.

Candy shrugs, spinning on her heel and heading toward a closet next to the couch. She slides the door open, and I get a good look at a large rack of costumes in a variety of holiday colors. "You look to be about a size four." It's not a question. She peeks at me over her shoulder, her eyes zeroing in on my belly. "Well, you used to be." My cheeks burn, not sure how to take that statement. Her eyes flick up to mine. She smirks. "Will be again in a few months. Until then, we'll make this work."

She pulls a green ensemble with white fur trim from the cabinet along with a small pink box. I watch as she settles at my feet and sets about preparing a sewing kit. My brows lift so high they hit my hairline. I swallow the last cracker, my mouth feeling dry once more.

"Does this mean I got the job?" I ask in shock.

Candy looks up at me, her eyes softer than they've been since I met her. "Of course you did. You need a job, and we've got them comin' out of our ears. Especially this time of the year. Hours and duties are flexible. Whatever you need, we'll make it happen."

"Why would you do that?" I blurt, unable to stop myself.

She grips my calf, squeezing it. "Why wouldn't I?"

I narrow my gaze at her, the answer obvious. "Because people don't do nice things for no reason. Everybody wants something."

Candy tuts, going back to her sewing kit. "Not in Jackson, we don't." I say nothing to that, and when it becomes clear my silence won't change, she continues. "I know you're new here, Tinsley Snow, but Jackson isn't like any other town you've ever been to. Good people live here. We're a community above everything else. We help our own." She lifts a slim shoulder. "Not to mention," she murmurs, looking up at me with a sly smirk. "I think this town needs you just as much as you need it."

Something in her gaze, or maybe her words, tells me that there's so much more to that statement than meets the eye. I don't comment on it, letting the comfortable silence fill the room once more. Candy spends almost half an hour tailoring a costume to fit me comfortably. When she finally finishes, my eyes are drifting closed, and I'm having a hard time standing upright.

"Bathrooms down the hall. First door on the right. It has a nice shower and is fully stocked with everything you'll need. Go take one and relax. Maybe nap on the couch when you're done. I'll bring you some lunch in an hour or so."

I open my mouth to argue. To tell her that's unnecessary. But my jaw immediately snaps shut when Candy gives me a long, sharp look, daring me to tell her no. I don't know why I would. A hot, free shower and a nap on a warm couch sound incredible right now. Not to mention, the idea of going back out to my freezing car makes me want to wither up in a ball and cry. So, I do something I haven't done in…ever.

I say yes, accepting someone's kindness with gratitude and appreciation instead of worrying about the repercussions of not doing everything myself.

Candy leaves me staring after her, my heart in my throat, my stomach filled with butterflies, and my soul lighter than it's been in years. Maybe Jackson, Wyoming, really is the place of Christmas miracles, after all.

# Chapter Four

## nicolai saint

"I UNDERSTAND WHERE YOU'RE coming from, Jameson, but I meant what I said. I'm stepping down. You and the board just need to come to terms with that," I state; no more fucks to give on the matter. A string of curses follows my declaration.

I press the mute button from my steering wheel and sigh heavily. I can't believe we're still having this conversation months after I decided to step down as CEO of the Saint Corporation. Who knew that when I started this company 23 years ago, I'd have to argue with thirty old men and women about my right to *quit my job*. It's ridiculous. Utterly insane.

Kevin Jameson is the lead director on my board, the biggest pain in my ass, and one of my oldest friends. He's also annoying me to no end. He groans loudly, and I roll my eyes, praying for some sort of divine intervention to save me from having to have this conversation yet again. Especially right now.

"Look," I say, unmuting the line as I pull into my spot near the back entrance of Wonderland. "I understand that this is an inconvenience for all of you, but it's not a shock, Kev. I told you guys four months ago that I'd be stepping down in the new year so I could focus on the Saint Foundation. I'm willing to work with you on appointing a new CEO. I will remain on the board. But I don't want this job anymore. It's time to move on."

He releases a heaving breath before falling into a coughing fit. I sit up straighter, not liking the sound of that at all. Kevin is well into his 80's. That's the only reason I didn't automatically make him the new Chief Officer of Wonderland Co. when I decided to hand it over and focus on my charity. Honestly, I think he's been waiting for me to make this move so he can finally retire. I know the pushback isn't coming from him but from the board.

When he gets ahold of himself, he responds, his voice raspy. "I know, son. I get it. I support you and what you're doing with those kids. I know you're ready to move on." He pauses, sounding like he's drinking something. Hopefully water. "You're a good man, Nico, but you're also an incredible businessman. The board's just worried about what will happen when you leave."

"Wonderland is built to last," I sigh, raking a hand through my hair. "As long as they don't change the business model or the way things are done, it will continue to succeed. If they run it into the ground, that's on them."

He makes a sputtering sound, and I grin, sliding from my car. "But it's your baby, Nicolai. How can you say that?"

I pause, my hand resting on the cold metal handle of the heavy back door. My brows pinch at his statement. "No," I murmur, shaking my head. "It's not. Not anymore."

"This business saved you. It pulled you from the streets. You built your entire life on Wonderland's back." He sounds appalled, and I don't blame him. "You're just willing to walk away. For what?"

"For life," I say, matter-of-factly. "I've dedicated almost 25 years to this company. It's time to move on. I have enough money. The company is set to thrive. I've already lost enough by putting it first." I shake away the thoughts of everything I've given up in the name of owning a successful company. Don't get me wrong—I wouldn't change anything. I've loved every second of building a good life, but in doing so, I've sacrificed actually living it. "I'm almost 50, Kev. I'm moving on. You guys need to as well."

With that, I hang up, leaving him to dissect my statement and, hopefully, inform the board that I'm not fucking around. They have less than six weeks to choose someone to take my place. After that, I'm done. I slide my phone into my pocket and head into the very company that, as Kevin put it, saved my life and pulled me from the streets.

I was born in a small town in Northern Wyoming. My parents were loving but struggled to maintain a roof over our heads for most of my childhood. When I was a teen, my father was killed in an accident, and my mother was never the same. She lost herself to drinking and drugs, following him to her death just years later. I was 16. I worked side jobs to pay for our tiny home, but the government found out I was an orphaned minor, pulled me from my shitty circumstances, and put me in foster care. Problem is, no one wants a teenager from the wrong side of the tracks. I was better off on my own, or so I thought.

I was homeless and in and out of shelters for almost a year. I traveled from town to town, working side jobs and saving what I could. It was hard. One of the hardest things I've ever done, but eventually, it paid off, and I found my way. One winter, I stumbled across a man named Ivan Saint. He was an elderly toy maker struggling to keep his shop open by himself. He offered me food and shelter in exchange for my help around his shop. I worked for him for years, learning the trade. When he passed, he left it all to me, including his last name. The rest is history.

As I step into the massive two-story building and take in the changes, I can't help but smile with pride and gratitude.

No. I don't take all the credit for my success over the last 23 years. I owe it all to Ivan. The man who took me in, clothed, and fed me when I needed it the most. The man who gave me everything and left with a valuable life lesson that, up until now, I've ignored.

*You can have all the money in the world, but you'll never be able to buy more time.*

I didn't understand him then. I was young. All I'd ever wanted was a comfortable life. A wife and family. Kids and enough money to look after them. But then, I was shown what grandeur looks like. I lost myself and my dreams. I was too busy chasing success and riches. Finally able to afford anything I could ever want and more. I thought I had it all. Hell, at one time, I even had that wife I'd dreamt of. But when she realized I wouldn't slow down... *couldn't* stop working, she found someone who would. I don't begrudge her for that. Leaving me and finding love elsewhere. But it was a wake-up call. So was the announcement of her wedding and first child. Then the second and third. That was 15 years ago. I started the Saint Foundation that same year.

If Ivan Saint saved me from the streets, then the foundation saved me from myself. Now, it's time to find my dreams and make them a reality...before it's too late.

The thought has me looking at my watch, then muttering a curse when I realize how behind I'm running. I need to find Candy, get my suit, and get to the hospital. Now. After searching the lower level and being stopped by customers and employees more times than I can count, I jog up the escalator, knowing she's more than likely in her office.

Candance, or Candy Cane as she's more aptly known around here, is my surrogate grandmother of sorts. After her husband passed ten years ago, she needed a hobby to occupy her time. Her love for children, despite never being able to have any of her own, led her to Wonderland. Or a sign from Santa, as she claims. Now, a decade later, she manages not only my store but my life as well. She looks after me and loves Wonderland like it's her own, to the point that she practically lives her. Hence, her office/apartment combo.

I reach her office in record time, my standing appointment at the children's hospital clanging through my mind like a church bell. I'm never late. Never. Not for them. But today, it seems, might be a first. Opening the door, I'm shocked when I find her space silent. Candy's obsessed with all things Christmas, music included.

"Candy?" I call out, letting the door close with a soft click behind me. When she doesn't respond, I realize it's her lunch hour, and she's likely over at The Frosty Spoon with her best friend, Lottie, as usual. I quickly make my way through the front room and down the hall to the fitting room, where she keeps our costumes. The door's closed. The rare sight has me slowing to a stop. I knock softly.

"Candace?" Nothing. Odd. Brows furrowed, I open the door and, once again, come to an immediate halt. "What the fuck?" I mutter.

There's a woman on Candy's couch if the long blonde hair fanning out over the nest of throw pillows is anything to go by. On silent feet, I pad over to the sofa and peer down at the sleeping stranger. My heart clenches painfully in my chest as I take her in. She's curled up on her side, facing the back of the couch. Her head is nestled into soft pillows, her body hidden beneath a pile of plush blankets, making it impossible to see her body. She's young. Pale skin, thick naturally red lips, nearly white hair that's damp. She snores softly, her chapped lips twitching in her sleep.

She's stunning. Fucking beautiful.

I bend over to get a better look, my hand resting on the couch above her. Who is she? Why is she here? Better yet...why does the sight of her make my brain short-circuit, my heart thump painfully, and my cock feel harder than it's ever been before?

She rolls onto her back, and I freeze, not moving an inch as I wait for her eyes to open, finding me mere inches from her face. I'm torn on whether or not I want that to happen. Part of me wants more than anything for her soft lids to peel back, showing me what I can only imagine are an incredible pair of eyes. *Blue.* I'd bet my life on her eyes being blue. Pure. Crystalline. Like her skin.

Seconds tick by, and nothing happens. She doesn't wake up, but the blankets do shift down her body as she gets comfortable. My mouth drops open. Pregnant. She's pregnant. *Very pregnant.* Emotions pound through me, clearing away the previous brain fog and creating a torrent of thoughts that are swirling too rapidly for me to understand. Anger at the sight of such a young woman being pregnant. Understanding that she's likely someone else's. Anger again at the thought of *that*...of her belonging to another man. Sadness as I take in the exhaustion beneath her eyes. The worn, stained clothing covering her small body and big belly. Irritation over the fact that despite her being another man's woman, my dick is still throbbing painfully in my slacks.

Her lips twitch again, this time turning upward in a soft smile. Another emotion. Need...need like I've never felt before. Need for her. Her smiles. Her name. Her story. Just *her.*

"Fuck," I choke out in a whisper. I shove away from the couch as though it's burned me. What I need is to get the hell out of here. Away from her. The unnamed siren threatening my existence. Threatening to send me into a tailspin. I have no idea what's happening to me right now. I just...I just need to go.

I spin on my heel, closing the distance between myself and the costume closet in less than a second. I rip one of my spare Santa suits from a hanger and then immediately berate myself when it clatters to the floor. I whirl around, my eyes wide, my heart lodged in my throat. The angel frowns in her sleep but doesn't wake up. Exhausted. *She's fucking exhausted.* The desire to go to her. Wrap her up. Keep her safe and cared for rises up inside me so fast I nearly groan. Shit. This is bad. More pissed off at myself than anything, I quietly leave the fitting room, closing the door behind me so she can continue to sleep.

I storm from the office, my hand raking through my hair repeatedly. I'm so lost in my thoughts I don't see Candy until I've run straight into her, knocking her onto the ground.

"Oh, shit," I grunt, bending down to help her up. Her eyes are wide, elf hat dangling precariously from her head, held on by one measly bobby pin.

Grimacing, I straighten her hat once she's steady on her feet. She bats my hands away when I try to brush off her outfit.

"What in the world has gotten into you?" she huffs, tugging down her green skirt.

I sigh, stepping away from her and collecting my Santa suit that I'd dropped in the chaos. I shake my head, not even sure where to start. Actually, that's not true. I know *exactly* what my problem is. My eyes flick over to the closed door at the end of the hall. My heart squeezes harshly, despising the hunk of wood between us.

Candy chuckles, dragging my attention from the door. I look down at her, unable to help myself from smirking at her elf costume. I may have always loved the holidays, an addiction that only grew once moving to Jackson, but it's Candance who initiated the Christmas theme at Wonderland. All the way down to the elf costumes and nicknames. It really does suit her, though.

"Oh, I get it," she laughs, her gray bob swishing with the movement. My eyes narrow in confusion. She shrugs, offering me a knowing look. "Met our new employee, did you?"

Employee? That's not good. Nope. Not good at all. I can't work with her. Correction...she can't work for me. That's a lawsuit waiting to happen if I've ever heard one.

Candy must see the panic in my eyes because her laughter stops. However, she doesn't stop grinning. If anything, she grins more. I swallow roughly. I want to tell Candy to fire the girl. Want to tell her to make sure I never see her again because if I do…well, I have no idea what will happen if I see her again. But it won't be good.

*Liar,* my brain supplies unhelpfully. *It will be amazing.* I scoff.

"Who is she?" I say instead, diverting my traitorous thoughts.

Candy's smile finally drops fully, taking my stomach along with it. She tuts, shaking her head as she sits down at her desk. "Her name is Tinsley Snow. She's 21 years old. Almost eight months pregnant. On the run from the child's father."

"Excuse me?" I snap. She shoots me an angry look, silently telling me to be quiet. I clench my jaw, rage damn near consuming me. I lean against the desk, my knuckles turning white from my grip, and hiss, "What happened?"

She eyes me, the deep frown lines around her mouth looking more harsh than usual. "It's not a good story, I fear, but I don't know the details, so—" The way her words trail off is suspicious as fuck, telling me she knows more than she's saying.

"Go on," I practically growl. She glares at me. We hold eye contact, a silent battle of wills happening between us. My muscles are tensed and ready for an invisible fight. I don't know why I'm reacting this way. I'm not normally a fighter, especially when it's not *my* fight to have. But this feels different. Fuck. I haven't even met her yet, and I'm already prepared to wage war on her behalf.

*Tinsley. Tinsley Snow.*

An angel.

Candance blinks rapidly, then rolls her eyes heavenward. "I don't know, Nico." I open my mouth to call her out, but a stern slash of her tiny hand through the air silences me. "I don't know what happened to her before she came to Jackson, but I do know she's been here for a few weeks." Her face takes on a severe look, and I already despise her next words. "Lottie says she lives in her car."

Fuck. That.

"No," is all I say in response, glowering down at Candy as though this entire situation is her fault, or maybe like she's the one who can fix it. I swallow. She *can* fix it. Actually...she already has, hasn't she? "You hired her? Officially?" She jerks a nod. "Is she staying here?" I gesture to the office. It's not a proper house, but it's better than a car. Yet, I still hate the idea of her being anywhere but with me. Christ. Candy hesitates. "Say it," I grunt, crossing my arms.

"She's here," she murmurs, pausing. "For now."

"What does that mean, Candance? She's not sleeping in her car. I won't have it."

Her thick brow arches. "Oh?" she drawls.

"Absolutely not."

I'm surprised when my words come out even instead of the loud battle cry I hear in my head. I stand to my full height, backing away a few steps. I really have to go. At this point, I'm so incredibly late that I have no doubt the hospital's panicking in my absence. I'm really never late, and I definitely never miss a volunteer shift. They're probably freaking the fuck out. Doesn't matter. This is more important.

*Holy shit.* I never thought I'd say that sentence or that I'd put something before the Saint Foundation. As the reality of that sinks in, further baffling me, I fall deeper into the confusion these last thirty minutes have brought on.

Candy continues to stare at me, waiting for me to speak. I don't know Tinsley whatsoever. Don't know a damn thing about her beyond the few facts that Candy just shared, yet the insatiable, indescribable need to protect her is consuming me right now.

"Is she safe?" I ask when the silence between us grows thick and unbearable. "From the baby's father?"

She smirks, a truly evil look taking over her usually sweet face. "He's dead."

My mouth drops open. That's not what I was expecting her to say. My shock quickly dissolves. Then, I'm smiling too. I want to ask how. Who he was and what happened, but it's pointless. I have absolutely no doubt in my mind that I'll be balls-deep in her history by midnight. I'll call a PI if I have to. I can already tell that no cost is too great when it comes to this woman.

Rolling my neck on my shoulders, I drop my hands and pick my Santa suit from the chair I'd abandoned it on. "She stays here until I can find a better place for her. She works as much as she wants. Takes all the breaks she needs. I'll take care of her checks myself." My gaze slides over to the fridge in the tiny kitchenette. I pull my company credit card from my wallet, dropping it onto the desk. "Stock the place with food. Drinks. Toiletries. Whatever she needs."

Candy lifts a brow and hides what I can only assume is a smirk or maybe a laugh behind her hand. "And how long should I plan on her being here? So I know how much food to buy."

I huff a breath. We both know that's not why she's asking. Doesn't matter. Turning toward the door, I call over my shoulder. "A week. Tops." Because after that, Tinsley Snow will be somewhere much safer than this old office. Like, with me. In my house. My mind drifts to her beautiful, swollen belly. I look back at Candy, finding her laughing silently. I roll my eyes. "Help her find a doctor in Jackson. Best one money can buy."

"She doesn't have money, Nico," she says softly, her voice serious.

I wave a dismissive hand. Tinsley now has access to as much money as she could ever want or need. "Sign her onto the company's insurance plan. Full benefits." I glance back at Tinsley's door one more time before leaving. "For both of them."

Because if the way my heart, brain, and dick are acting is anything to go by, Tinsley Snow and her baby are about to become Saints. And Saints take care of their own.

Maybe I should have told Candy to book me a CAT scan while she was at it because, clearly, I've gone insane.

# Chapter Five

## TINSLEY SNOW

A WEEK PASSES, AND I find myself settling happily into my new job and Jackson as though it was always meant to be. I'm still absorbing the shock of Vincent's death. After running for so long. Constantly looking over my shoulder and waiting for the other shoe to drop, it's difficult to just...*be*. But the epic whirlwind this last week has helped me move forward, putting Vincent and my past behind me.

Last week, when I'd stumbled from the shower Candy had basically demanded I take, I'd passed out. Hard. So hard that I slept for over ten hours. Only waking when it felt as though my bladder was going to explode, and my stomach was gnawing through my organs, searching for food. Pixie, no doubt, behind both of those issues. It took work to pull myself from the couch and the beautiful dreams I'd been having, but when I did, I was shocked at what I found.

Candy was sitting on a chair across from me, sleeping under a blanket with a forgotten book on her lap. Next to her, on a small coffee table, was what appeared to be a five-course meal from Lottie and Oscars. Next to that was a large stack of new clothes. Women's, and all in my size. A new pair of boots sat in a department store box, as well as gloves, scarves, and a puffy, warm winter coat. My elf shoes on top of them. Lastly was my Wonderland costume. Perfectly tailored and smelling of baby detergent. I cried. Loudly. Loud enough to wake Candy with a startle. She simply smiled, told me to eat up and get to work before disappearing from the office.

It was difficult to accept her hospitality and the overwhelming generosity of her gifts. The food, toiletries, clothes. *The apartment.* But then, I remembered Lottie's words about the people at the shelter and then Oscar helping her. Saving her. I needed that. I still do. Accepting help and handouts has been one of the most difficult things for me to do. Yet, even if I survived living out of my car for months, it's not the life I want for my child. So, I swallowed my pride, choked down the metaphorical milk and cookies, and vowed to earn my keep, which has surprisingly been easier than I thought.

"Did you call the doctor yet?" Lottie asks, leaning over the checkout counter I'm stationed at for the next half-hour. She's come in to see me at Wonderland almost daily. Buying my affection with pancakes, hamburgers, and milkshakes. Not that she needs to.

I bend over, stretch my back out, and nod before realizing she can't see me. I stand up, groaning and palming my lower back. Thoughts of what a woman with money, or hell, a comfortable bed, might be doing at 35 weeks pregnant flit through my mind. I have no doubt that pregnancy aches are normal, but I'm sure it doesn't have to hurt quite *this* badly. Unlike a lot of women, I've loved being pregnant. It's been a beautiful journey, despite how it began. I love knowing Pixie is happy and safe, growing inside of me. I love the changes I see in my body. The way I feel. It's truly one of the most incredible experiences of my life.

But...carrying around a bowling ball is hard. Especially when standing all day.

Lottie sighs in frustration, joining me behind the counter. She pushes the chair Candy got me towards my ass, practically shoving me into a seated position. I glare up at her but sink into the soft cushion anyways. My body practically cries out with relief.

"They bought you that thing for a reason, *Tinsel Toes*." She falls into a fit of giggles, laughing at my expense, repeating my new elf name repeatedly. I shake my head and push her away from me with a growl. "Oh, come on now, little one. Don't get your tinsel in a tangle. You'll make Santa sad."

"Fuck off," I snap, but there's no heat behind it. A quiet gasp drags my attention from a still-laughing Lottie to a tiny elf on my left. Her cheeks are pink, her mouth hanging open in shock. I cringe. "Sorry, Pipsqueak," I murmur, feeling awful. "I wasn't talking to you. I promise."

She closes her mouth, nodding once. "Okay," she whispers. "I just came to let you know we have an elf meeting in thirty minutes. Candy Cane asked me to tell everyone. Mr. Saint will be here." She blushes, looking down at her toes.

Poor girl. Pipsqueak, or Penelope, is the girl I met on my first day here. She is, in fact, only in High School, as I'd assumed, but she's younger than I thought at only 14. Apparently, along with his long list of good deeds, Mr. Saint also employs foster kids who need a helping hand. He doesn't pay them an actual wage unless they're over 16, but he does give them stipends for food, clothes, and other necessities, as well as a safe place to hang out.

I've yet to meet the man, but at this point, there's no doubt in my mind that he's an actual, literal saint.

"Yeah, Pip," Lottie adds softly. "Our little Tinsel Toes just needs a snack. Then she'll be bright and jolly for your staff—I mean elf meeting."

Penelope smiles brightly and skips away, embracing the costume like a real-life elf. It's adorable. Lottie pulls the milkshake she'd brought me out from beneath the counter where I stashed it and hands it to me with a stern look.

"You need to eat something, and for God's sake, Tinsley, use the damn chair. If they didn't want you to sit, they wouldn't have given it to you." I groan but suck the straw into my mouth and nod.

"Now," she tuts, tapping her toe. "Did you make the appointment to see Dr. Talbot or not?"

I swallow half the shake, Pixie dancing with joy at the sugar rush. "Yes. I see her next week at Gresham General," I say, speaking of the major hospital in town.

Dr. Talbot is apparently the best obstetrician and gynecologist in all of Wyoming. When I'd told Lottie and Candy that I didn't mind going to the local free clinic, they'd both gasped as though I'd said I'll be delivering Pixie in my car. Candy merely shoved a business card and insurance information into my hands before turning and leaving me to gape after her. Never in my life have I heard of a job giving you full benefits that include doctors' visits, pre, and post-natal care, dental, vision, and a variety of other services...all completely free. It's mind-boggling, but I know better than to look a gift horse in the mouth.

"Good." Lottie smiles, tucking an errant strand of hair behind my ear as she looks down at me with pride. She's become somewhat of a makeshift mom to me these last few weeks. I appreciate her more than I can say. Affection and joy fill me as I reflect on how much my life has changed since I found this sweet town. I don't know how things can get any better than they are right now. "And have you met Mr. Saint yet?"

I finish off my shake, toss the empty cup in the trash, and stand, the mention of my new boss reminding me of the tasks I need to finish before the meeting. "No," I grunt, the baby kicking my ribs as I shift. "Candy said he was in board meetings all week, which I assume is normal for him."

I lift a shoulder, opening the register to do the end-of-the-day cash count. Wonderland closed a half hour ago, and everything's nearly shut down for the evening. Lottie snickers, rounding the counter to give me space. She digs through her purse, pulling out a clear makeup bag. I watch her out of the corner of my eye, my nose scrunched up when she digs out a selection of lip glosses that don't match her complexion. She flicks her eyes from me to the tubes, back and forth, before settling on a light red color with a nod.

"That doesn't match your hair, Lott," I murmur, sliding the stack of bills into an envelope for Candy. Lottie doesn't say anything as she leans over the counter and tugs me forward softly. I screech, making sure my bump doesn't hit the hard wooden edge. "What the hell?"

She clicks her tongue. "This isn't for me."

That's the only warning I get before she's covering my already red lips in a sticky gloss. Within minutes, my previously blank face is highlighted, blushed, glossed, and mascaraed. I do nothing, too shocked to object and too giddy at the feeling of wearing makeup for the first time in months to complain. When she's done, she claps, happy with her work.

"Perfect." She tucks her makeup bag away and throws her purse over her shoulder before giving me a serious look. "Just remember, Tinsley Snow. You're a badass and a survivor, but you're also a woman who deserves nothing but the best." I swallow a messy ball of emotions, her words catching me off guard. "You and Pixie don't have to be alone if you don't want to be."

With that ominous declaration, she turns toward the exit, tossing, "Don't forget to smile," over her shoulder as she goes. I stare after her for a long moment, losing myself to my thoughts. Before I know it, Penelope's back, letting me know it's time for the meeting. I exhale a rough breath, my heart aching in my chest and my belly rolling with nerves. Why? I don't know. But something about Lottie's words have me feeling incredibly emotional.

Tucking the cash envelope into the safe, I slip from behind the register and follow the rest of the employees toward the break room. Everyone is chattering adamantly about their weekend plans. Most of the staff is younger than me, but there are a few people my age and older. A couple are even Candy's age, which I've now learned is 61. I offer them smiles but can't shake the feeling of nervous anticipation raking over my skin.

I find a seat toward the front, happy it's not the low couch that I'd no doubt struggle to crawl from after the meeting. Looking around, I'm surprised by how many people have crowded into the large room. Everyone came in for this meeting, so it's my first time seeing the whole staff at once. I guess it makes sense. You'd need a lot of people to work in such a huge store, especially during the holidays.

"Okay, everyone," Candy says, gaining my attention. She smiles sweetly, her usual costume perfectly in place as usual. "Thank you all for coming. We have a few things to get through before the Thanksgiving break." I swallow, my eyes widening. I'd completely forgotten that Thanksgiving is in three days. "But first, Mr. Saint is here with a couple of announcements."

Cheers ring out through the room as a man wearing a fancy black suit stands from the row of chairs directly in front of me. I hadn't even noticed him in all of the chaos. My heart speeds up at the reaction from the staff. He really is loved here. No, not just here. In Jackson as a whole. I feel like I'm about to meet a celebrity or…well…or Santa. I smile, the excitement from everyone around me infectious.

He turns around.

My smile drops. My heart skips a beat. Then another. My stomach twists, and my palms begin to sweat. My mouth goes dry. I feel like I'm dying and living for the first time all at once. And then, he speaks. His voice is deep and raspy, as though he's been talking all day. It's soft. Kind. Beautiful.

"For those of you who don't know me, my name is Nicolai Saint." He turns his gaze toward me, staring directly into my eyes as though he's searching for my soul. "But, please, call me Nico."

His eyes stay locked onto mine. Everything and everyone around me disappears except for him. *Nicolai Saint.* The most gorgeous man I have ever seen in my entire life. My clit throbs in time with my rapidly beating heart. My world shifts on its axis. And then…he smiles at me.

Oh, fuck.

# Chapter Six

## TINSLEY SNOW

T IME STANDS STILL AS we stare at each other. It feels as though his words and attention are just for me. Someone coughs. Nico shifts, his eyes narrowing before seemingly shaking himself out of his stupor. His brows dip in confusion. I see the exact moment the room, the people, and the meeting all come back to him. It's about the same time as they do for me. *Holy hell.* How long were we just staring at each other? And why?

That was insane. I've never had a reaction like that to a man in my life. I've seen gorgeous men before, but they've never elicited that kind of response from me or my body. I feel like I got caught in a rainstorm and was standing too close to a lightning strike.

I'm still dissecting what just happened when Mr. Saint—Nico...begins to speak. He looks confident but slightly rattled, bracing his hands behind his back. "As you all know, with the holidays, things around here will be extremely busy and chaotic. Like every year, we will continue to offer triple time for anyone who *chooses* to work this next week, as well as the week of Christmas."

His emphasis on the word *chooses* doesn't escape me. Candy had already explained that it's completely optional to be here or with your families for the holidays. Staff can take paid time off without repercussion, but there are incentives to work. I just hadn't realized it was so much money on the table. I'd already offered to be here, knowing I had nowhere else to go, but that kind of cash...*wow*.

I could do so many things. I'd be that much closer to an apartment of my own. A real bed. A crib for Pixie. *I need to do better for her.* I rub my belly, needing the connection and reminder that she's happy, safe, and healthy right now. *I'm doing my best*, I mentally chide. I'm trying to be kinder to myself, but it's hard after so many years of beating myself up. I grimace at the thought.

"Tinsley?" a masculine voice calls. My eyes snap up, finding everyone looking at me, Nico and Candy included. I blink rapidly, confused as hell about what I missed. His brows are drawn in tight, his expression soft and filled with concern. It's the complete opposite of his posture. His hands are clenching and unclenching at his sides. His muscles are rigid, and his body is leaning toward me as though he's holding himself back.

"Yes?" I ask quietly, hugging my belly tighter.

His eyes widen a fraction, dropping down to where I'm cradling my stomach. He swallows, his jaw flexing. "Are you okay?" His voice is different. Deeper. Gravely.

Confused, I nod before glancing at Candy. Her eyes flicker between Nico and me, a wide smirk on her face. It only serves to baffle me more.

"You looked like you were in pain," he says with a slightly awkward laugh. "I—*we* were worried about you." I nearly gasp. Not only does this man know my name, but he was worried...about me? Either I'm low on sugar or dreaming because there is no way any of this is happening to me right now. Maybe I froze over in my car, and this is Heaven.

But the uncomfortable stares of dozens of people penetrating into me from all sides prove that it's most definitely not. I lean back, trying to appear as though I'm calm and collected. Not panicked and sweaty with a healthy dose of freaking the fuck out. Remembering Lottie's words, I smile. Nico jolts back like I've slapped him. My smile wilts, and I immediately wonder if there's something in my teeth.

"Anyways," Candy drawls, huffing a laugh. "Now that we all know Tinsley is well, let's get back to the meeting. I've got a hot date in an hour with Marty Merryfingers from packing, and I don't want to be late."

Everyone makes sounds that remind me of when my classmates found out about my crush on Ben Wheeler in sixth grade. Women giggle as they turn to a tall, grey-haired, blushing man leaning against the back wall. He looks mortified, but his eyes are sweet as they take in Candy.

"Merryfingers," someone fake-coughs, turning the low chuckles into raucous laughter.

Nico shoots Candy an odd look, as though he's struggling to compose himself, before finally continuing. For some reason, he's becoming more and more frazzled the longer this meeting goes on. Good. At least I'm not the only one.

"Right," he chuckles awkwardly, running his hand through his thick hair. "As I was saying. You're welcome to work, get paid the incentive, or stay home with your families. Either way, we'll cover things here so you can enjoy your holidays. There is also an opportunity to work extra hours if you'd like to. My charity, the Saint Foundation, will be attending local hospitals, shelters, and orphanages over the next six weeks. Just like every year, I'll be dressed as Santa, and who is Santa without his elves?"

A round of laughter follows his cheery declaration. I find myself leaning forward in my chair, enthralled by his commanding presence and gorgeous smile.

Nico is a tall man, at least 6'0, but he's not large. He's thin, yet even beneath his suit, I can tell he's muscular. Every time he shifts, claps, or squeezes the table behind him, his biceps flex, causing the fitted black material to tighten. His hair is dark brown but streaked with grey, particularly at his temples. His skin is slightly darker than mine. His face is covered in a closely cropped salt-and-pepper beard. Fine lines wink in and out at the corners of his lips and eyes when he laughs or smiles.

He's distinguished. Professional yet...jolly? I don't even know if that's a way you're supposed to describe a man. Especially one like *him*, but it's the only thing I can think of to describe his aura. When Nicolai Saint laughs, you can tell he feels it down to his bones. It's intoxicating. So much so that as he continues to talk, joking with a few of his employees, I find myself smiling and chuckling along with him. Craving more of his warm spirit. More of *him*.

He stands up straight, bracing his hands on his hips. "Lastly, I wanted to apologize for how absent I've been over the last week. I know you're all used to seeing me here with you every day, manning the floors and customer crowds alongside you. Now that my meetings are over, I'll be back in the trenches starting tomorrow." His eyes find mine again, a heated look in them that almost has me falling to my knees and choking on my tongue. "So, you can expect to see a lot more of me. I'm not going anywhere."

Again...why does it feel like he's speaking directly to *me*? I don't even know him. Nico turns away from me, clapping once and smiling widely.

"I'm going to turn the meeting back over to Candy Cane so we can get her out of here on time for her date." Everyone catcalls, making Candy blush. "Don't forget. Sign-ups for the charity meet and greets with Santa, and his elves are on the bulletin board in the back. First shift is Thanksgiving." He swallows, his Adam's apple bobbing as he glances at me a final time. "I hope to see your name on it."

That was most definitely directed at me. Before I can respond, not that I would know what to say, Nico is already gone.

# Chapter Seven

## nicolai saint

"OKAY, EVERYONE. CALM DOWN," I grunt, shoving the herd of beasts away from me. Seven sets of sad eyes meet mine as they drop down onto their haunches and whimper. I sigh but can't help the smile creeping over my lips as I try to remain stern. Wagging my finger useless, I shake my head. "You need to behave for the sitter today." I shoot a glare over at the smallest of the pack, my hands on my hips. "That means you, Prancer. I'm not fucking around here. Do not, and

I mean, *do not,* drag Penny through the park again today."

I didn't know it was possible, but I swear, the Pomeranian rolls his eyes at me. I scoff. Prancer lets out a little growl that wouldn't even scare a kitten but somehow makes him puff up as though he's a Doberman. I click my tongue in disapproval and look over the rest of the bunch.

"I have to go to work today, which means we won't see the kids until Thanksgiving." I glance down at my watch, my face twitching with a smirk when I notice it's nearly 10:00 am. Showtime. I flick my gaze back to the raggle-taggle bunch of dogs that I've accumulated over the last five or so years, and my heart fills with pride. They really are good dogs. I scowl at Prancer again. "Except for you. You're a little shi—"

"Hello, Mr. Saint," a tiny voice chirps, luckily interrupting me. The dogs lose their shit, noticing the newcomer, running from me as though I'm not the man who literally saved them from death. I bark out a laugh as they take her to the ground, covering her in kisses. She giggles freely, looking more relaxed than I usually see her. It warms my heart to no end.

Penelope, or Pipsqueak, is a super sweet kid that works at Wonderland. She has a fucked up home life, a story I don't even fully know, and often needs a safe place to hang out. Legally, I can't *hire* her as an employee since she's so young. But I can pay her to walk my dogs and watch them while I work.

Sliding my hands into my pockets, I shift back on my heels, the desire to run all the way to The Frosty Spoon now that Penn is here filling me rapidly. I smile, offering her a nod. "Nice to see you, Pipsqueak." She blushes, and I chuckle quietly. It would take a blind man not to notice her crush on me. It's cute but also awkward as fuck. She's so young, and technically, I'm her boss.

*A rule I clearly don't apply to everyone.* I nearly scoff. *Yeah. I'm going nuts here.*

"Everyone's been fed. They're ready for their wa—" I grimace. "They're ready," I amend. Everyone knows you never say the word walk around a hyper dog. Especially seven of them.

She huffs, shoving them off of her and climbing to her feet, still smiling. "Does Dasher need his ear medicine?" I nod. She jots a note on her phone. "And what about Vixen? Has he had his antibiotics yet today?"

I look down at my sweet boy. Vixen is a Pitbull and my most recent adoption. I rescued him from an illegal dog fighting ring the police shut down. His small size and disposition clearly weren't suited for the god-awful practice if his scars were anything to go by. After having him checked over by doctors, we worked with a trainer to ensure he fully recovered from his hard life and would be safe to be around kids. He passed with flying colors. Unfortunately, some of his wounds will take much longer to heal. Even a warm bed and love can't fix the deepest injuries.

"I changed his bandages this morning, but he got sick after he took his pills. The vet said to try again this afternoon." She gives him a sad look before dropping back down to fawn over him, making sure to be gentle with the thick bandages around his left eye and ear. Poor guy. "I have to take off, Penn. Call me if you need anything. Lunch is in the fridge for you. I should be back around five." She waves me off, not even saying goodbye before cooing at the dogs.

I smile, my heart racing wildly as I take off for my car. It's been a week since I learned of Tinsley Snow's existence. My reaction to her only solidified my decision to step down from Wonderland Co. Unfortunately, that required me to spend a week in back-to-back meetings. It worked out, I suppose. It gave it time to acclimate and settle into her new life here in Jackson. It also gave me time to make my preparations.

Jogging to the front door, my eyes flick to the staircase and toward the second floor of my home as though I can see the new editions I've made through the walls. I smile widely. I can't wait for Tinsley to see them. Now, all I need to do is convince her to fall for me, move in with me, and accept her new future...as my wife and mother of my children.

As I said. I've completely lost my mind.

Oh well. They say the first step is admitting you have a problem. And my problem is that I've become utterly obsessed with Tinsley Snow.

*Mine.*

The overhead bell rings as I step into The Frosty Spoon. A few people notice me immediately, waving to say hello. I smile, shaking hands and making small talk, fighting the urge to let my eyes wander.

I've tried to get them to stop. The town. My friends. I love everyone in Jackson. This town has become more than a home to me. But I'm not the mayor. I'm not anyone of power or a government official. Hell, I'm no one. Just a rich bastard from the slums who found solace in a tiny town as a homeless teenager. My money doesn't make me important. If anything, I'd rather be recognized for the charity work I do and not for the reasons people think. If they know about the Saint Foundation, people are more likely to help out where they can. Giving back doesn't require money, just a heart and desire to make things better. That's all I want for Jackson.

I squeeze Harriet's shoulder as I pass by her and finally give in to the desire to look around. To look for *her*. It's Tinsley's day off, and if my slightly creepy sleuthing is anything to go by, she should be here. I try to be discreet as I make my way to my usual table in the back. It's been a while since I've had time to stop in for a meal here, but I try to frequent local businesses as much as possible. I freeze in place as I find my table occupied. It's not that someone is sitting there. I don't really care about that. I don't own the damn thing.

No. It's *who's* sitting there.

I swallow the immediate ball of nerves that clogs my throat as I take in her beautiful profile. She's so fucking beautiful. The most incredible woman I've ever seen in my life. Everything about her is...beautiful.

My eyes dip down to the wide swell of her belly, and emotion like I've never felt before barrels into me. Anger at the circumstances revolving around the baby's conception. The details my PI found that first night she drifted into my life. The man responsible for Tinsley's pain, heartache, and likely why she was on the run in the first place. Thank god the bastard's already dead or else I'd have to make peace with a prison sentence because I'd no doubt be sent away for murder. I force down the anger clawing at my insides on focus on the here and now. My mind immediately fills with questions that I have no right to ask but can't possibly put a stop to.

*Is the baby okay?*
*How are you feeling?*
*Do you need anything?*
*Is it a boy or a girl?*
*Do they have a name?*

A soft throat clearing draws my attention to the very confused but blushing woman who is undoubtedly wondering why and the absolute fuck a strange man is staring at her pregnant belly. Oh, shit.

*Get it together, Nico. Don't be such a fucking creep.*

I smile, stepping forward and closing the distance between us. Her long, white-blonde hair is up today in a messy bun, exposing the long column of her neck. She's wearing a thick cream sweater that looks cozy and warm as it dwarfs her small body. My chest burns at the realization that it's one of the pieces of clothing I bought her. Not that she knows it, but I couldn't help it. She needed new clothes that fit her. Kept her and the baby warm. And the thought of anyone else buying them for her, providing for her...it made me slightly murderous.

"Uh," she murmurs, clearing her throat again. "Did you need something?"

*And I'm staring again.* Fucking hell. You'd think I'm an inexperienced teenage boy instead of a divorced 46-year-old man.

"How are you, Tinsley?" I ask, my voice catching on her name. Her eyes widen slightly, her light cheeks turning bright pink for some reason.

She swallows, sitting up straighter in her chair. Pride fills me at the sight of it. My girl is a fighter. "I'm great, actually. How are you, Mr. Saint?"

Holy fucking hell. Why does the sound of *her* using my full in that way make my cock instantly harden? Normally I despise being called something so formal. In fact, I generally encourage everyone, including the board, to call me Nico. But when Tinsley says it, it elicits visions of me fucking her on her hands and knees, shouting my name as she cums all over my cock.

Shit. Now I'm the one blushing. I shift, needing to hide my obvious erection. I point to the empty chair across from her and arch a brow. "Is it okay if I join you? And please, call me Nico."

*Or don't. Whatever.*

I really hope she says yes because I'm going to look like a crazy person when I do it anyways, no matter her answer. Tinsley pauses, her hand hanging limply in the air as she reaches for what appears to be a Christmas explosion in a cup. She tugs her fat bottom lip between her teeth, and my already hard cock throbs angrily. She nods. I don't waste a second, needing to hide my dick beneath the table more than I need air. I slide my charcoal peacoat off, leaving me in dark jeans and a long-sleeved black sweater. I drop down into the chair, my body tensing for the inevitable awkwardness that's about to hit the both of us.

She cocks her head to the side, her delicate fingers wrapping around her cup as she looks me over. I barely resist the urge to flex my muscles. Her lip twitches, and her eyes, which are every bit as crystal blue as I knew they'd be, twinkle.

"How many dogs do you have?" Her question throws me for a loop. My mouth drops open, and my brows pinch. That's not what I was expecting her to say at all.

Before I can answer, Harriet's delivering a cup of coffee for me along with a tiny pitcher of milk and a plate of oatmeal raisin cookies. My favorite. I thank her, not missing the way her gaze darts between the two of us, a knowing look plastered across her aging face. I roll my eyes but smirk, turning back to Tinsley just as she takes a sip of her concoction.

"Why do you ask that?" I finally respond.

She sets up the cup down, her tongue darting out to clean up the creamy white mess left behind from the whipped cream. I swear to God, my dick jumps to attention and hits the bottom of the table at the sight. Somehow, without even trying, she's sex personified. Pregnant belly and all.

My eyes drop down as if to check on the baby again, but they catch on her full, large breasts, which are barely contained beneath the thick sweater. I have to lift my coffee to hide my groan. I bet they're beautiful. Her pale skin is probably stretched to its limit, heavy with milk to feed her baby. My mouth salivates, and I choke on a large swallow of steaming coffee. Tinsley panics, pushing to stand, but I wave her away, not wanting her to come any closer. Not right now. If I see her up close, smell her, I'll straight up keel over.

She settles, giving me an odd look as I try to process what the fuck just happened. That was new...like, really new. I love boobs just as much as the next man, but I've never thought about a woman's milky tits before. Definitely never craved them. Their flavor. The feeling of the warm liquid sliding down my throat. I bet it's sweet as hell. Tinsley shifts. Her breasts press together and create all sorts of wild visions in my head.

My cock covered in her breastmilk, sliding between the heavy swells. Her tongue out and lapping up my precum with every pass.

Me fucking her from behind, my hands palming her belly lovingly while milk trickles down her chest.

Her riding me, my mouth latched to a red, pointed nipple as I suck her flavor down my throat.

My eyes widen in shock as my heart races painfully in my chest.

New kink...*unlocked.*

# Chapter Eight

## nicolai saint

OH, FUCK. I SHAKE my head, clearing my throat once more before locking my gaze firmly where it belongs. Her eyes.

*Her eyes, Nico. Focus, man.*

We stare at each other for countless seconds, maybe longer. I lose myself there, in her eyes. She really is stunning. But more than that, I see a kinship in Tinsley's features. The tired bags under her eyes have all but disappeared in the last week, showing how much a warm place to sleep and a steady diet have helped her. I know it's more than that, though. It's the stability. The job, money, and running water. The not having to worry about where you'll sleep that night or how you'll get your next meal. It's consistency. Safety. It's having a place to rest your head at night and people to catch you when you fall.

It's people to help keep you standing in the first place.

I know because I was Tinsley. I may not have been on the run after an assault the way she was. I may not have been raped or impregnated, and God knows what else, but I was broken. I was terrified and alone. I was *cold*. People who have never known what being truly starving and freezing feels like could never understand. But I do. Maybe that's why I'm drawn to her so much. Maybe that's why I can't force myself to pull away from her.

Maybe that's why I don't want to.

"You're sweater," she says softly, pulling me from my heavy thoughts. I blink rapidly, my brows dipping in confusion. Her thick lips tilt up, a mischievous glint in her eyes that I immediately know I'll crave more of after this. "Your sweater is covered in dog hair. Didn't you notice?"

It takes a moment for her words to compute, but when they do, I glance down, taking in my black shirt. Sure enough, there's enough hair on me to build an eighth dog to add to my pack. I groan, squeezing my eyes shut and shaking my head. Embarrassment coats my skin, and that's not something I've felt in a long time. But I wanted to make a good impression on Tinsley.

She giggles, pulling my attention to her mouth for the thousandth time. I release of huff of air that's meant to be light but comes out breathy. There goes that bottom lip between her teeth again. I'm never going to make it out of this alive, am I?

"Sorry about that," I murmur, my meaning layered.

She shrugs, releasing her lip with a pop. "How many do you have? Dogs, I mean."

"Seven," I say offhandedly. She gasps, making me chuckle. "What would Santa be without his reindeer?" Tinsley leans forward, dropping her elbows to the table before propping her head up on her tiny fists. Cute. She's so fucking cute.

"Well, go on," she practically begs. I like the sound of that far too much. *Focus, Nico.* "You can't drop a line like that and not finish your story."

Running a hand through my hair, I mirror her position. "I have seven rescued dogs that I dress up like reindeer and take with me on charity events." Her eyes soften a fraction, slowly drawing me in closer. "I wear my Santa costume. Elves from Wonderland volunteer to come with me, and we pass out gifts to children in orphanages, foster homes, and hospitals. Or." I break off, tipping my shoulder. "Whoever needs some cheering up."

She looks like she might cry, and I immediately want to bundle her up. "But," she whispers. "Doesn't Santa have eight reindeer?"

I nod, a pang of sadness making itself known in my chest next to all of the overwhelming happiness she inspires. "Rudolph passed away a few months ago. I haven't had the heart to replace him yet."

"Shit," she gasps.

Her hand darts out, squeezing my forearm as she offers me her condolences. My heart rate picks up...over just her touch. Her tiny fingers wrapping around my arm has me nearly fainting in the best way. Tinsley sucks in a sharp breath, realizing what she's done, and moves to pull away. I refuse to allow that. I can't. I grab her retreating hand, wrapping it in mine. She makes a tiny whimpering sound but doesn't try to fight my grip. It's not hard. She could pull away if she wanted to. But I make my intention clear.

Surprisingly, she settles immediately, sinking into the feeling of her hand being held by my much larger one. It dwarfs hers. I like that. I like it *a lot*.

"It's okay," I say quietly, again, giving her a double meaning with my words.

She swallows thickly before shocking the hell out of me when she threads our fingers together. Now there's no way to misinterpret what this means. We may have just met. We may be truly speaking for the first time right now, but I can't deny what my body feels near hers. My soul, my heart. It knows. I just hope hers does as well.

Trying to bring us back to the previous topic, I ask the first thing that comes to mind. "Do you have any pets?" I immediately berate myself for such a callous question. Her eyes gloss over, telling me exactly what I need to know. She did, but she gave it up when she ran. "Fuck, Tinsley, I'm so sorry. I should have known better."

Her hand shifts as she tries to pull away, needing the distance between us as her emotions swell. I want nothing more than to refuse her. To be here for her. To comfort her. But, after what she's been through, I can't do that with touch. Not yet.

She leans back in her chair, her hands immediately going to her baby bump. I watch her trace idle patterns across it, her eyes getting lost as she looks over my shoulder. I don't look, though, too consumed by the way she touches her bump. Can she feel the baby right now? Does the baby know how much its mama loves them?

My hands ache with the need to feel what she's feeling. I squeeze my eyes shut and lean back, granting her more distance. I'm an idiot for believing this would be simple.

"I had a cat. Her name was Stella. I had to leave her with a neighbor when I ran." She gives me a strange look, her head cocking to the side in that way of hers. "I ran because my ex-boss assaulted me while I was at work." She pauses, her words almost sounding like a threat. Maybe a warning. I'm also not so stupid as to ignore the resemblance between her past and present. The difference is—I would never, and I mean *never*, touch her without her consent. "But something tells me you already knew that."

My palm finds my rough, short beard. I can't deny it. I do know about her past. Likely more than anyone else, but not for long. I nod. "This town is small, Tinsley." I'm not going to admit I hired a PI to dig into her records, but I won't lie, either. "I know what happened. How you came to be in Jackson."

Her eyes tear up. I hate it. I hate it so much that I lose my battle with holding back. I stand slowly, thankful that the sight of her crying immediately had my dick welting. I round the table, coming to her side. I dip down into a crouch, completely ignoring the people around us. I want to hold her face. Want to wipe away her tears. But I don't. I don't touch her. I just have this overwhelming need to comfort her. It's clear that she's been alone for a long time. Whether it's me or someone else, I don't want her to have to go through this alone. But—I will likely lose my shit if it's not *me* holding her when she'd ready.

Tinsley shifts away from me, her wet eyes wide as she stares down at me below her. Before she can really freak out, I speak, hoping to calm her.

"I may know the details, but I don't know everything, Tinsley. I don't know what you've been through or how much you've had to endure by yourself, but I do know you don't have to anymore." I want to leave it there. Want to tell her I'm here now, but I can see her retreating. Can see the panic on her pretty face. I swallow. "Jackson is a good, safe town filled with wonderful people. You never have to be alone again. You can have friends here. A family." My eyes search hers, unable to leave that last part out. "You can have it all." I flick my gaze down to her baby, my hand literally throbbing with need. "You both can."

We sit in silence. I should move. Should sit down. But I can't. Not yet. She exhales roughly. I jump when I feel her hand land on my shoulder. I glance up at her. She's smiling. Crying but smiling. "Thank you, Nico."

"He's right, you know," a raspy female voice adds softly. We both jump, finding Lottie staring down at us, a loving expression on her face as she watches our interaction. "You're not alone, Darlin'. Neither is Pixie. You both have a home here for as long as you like." Her eyes flick to mine. She tuts once but smiles. "You have a family here." She looks back at Tinsley, her gaze almost imploring her to see what's right in front of her. "If you want it. All you have to do is say yes."

With that, she turns, leaving us alone once more. I push to my feet, giving in to one more need. I bend over and press a kiss to the top of Tinsley's head. It's brief. Only long enough to give me a hit of her intoxicating scent and hear her breathy gasp. I smile into her soft hair before stepping away and retaking my seat. I look down, finding pancakes on the table in front of both of us, and laugh. I really do lose track of my surroundings when we're together.

I dig in, not looking at Tinsley, so I don't call attention to what I just said and did. When I finally see her begin to eat out of the corner of my eye, I start talking again. "Pixie?"

I hear her swallow but keep my gaze on my plate. The pancakes here are incredible. "It's what I call the baby."

My. Fucking. Heart. I pause, unable to resist meeting her eyes. I damn near choke on my food. "It's a girl?" Why does my voice sound like I got kicked in the balls? "The baby is a girl?" I repeat dumbly.

She blushes, shaking her head before digging back in. She shovels a large bite of food into her mouth, moaning as it reaches her tastebuds. Christ, have fucking mercy.

"No," she murmurs, washing down her food with what I can see is coffee now that the whipped cream has dissolved. I glare at it. I may or may not have consumed every baby and pregnancy book I could get my hands on in the last week. I know caffeine is bad for babies. "I don't know how to describe it. I just know."

I look up, finding her giving me a bashful look. My glare withers away. "So," I nod. "Pixie is a girl," I agree. Her smile is huge as she nods. I can't help but smile back. "And is Pixie the official name?" It's not what I would have picked, but who am I to judge? That baby will be gorgeous, just like her mama. We can call her whatever Tinsley likes if it keeps her smiling like that. "I love it."

She snickers, diving back into her food. "It's just a nickname," she says with a mouthful of eggs. I'm thankful Lottie's forcing her to eat more protein, a fact I also heard through the grapevine. What can I say? Santa has elves everywhere. "Do you have any kids? A wife?"

I don't miss the awkward way she stares at her plate or the lilt in her voice as she prods for info. I could fall to my knees again and weep. She wants to know about me? *Perfect.* I could fuck around. Toy with her. But something tells me that's not what Tinsley needs right now.

"Nope," I say, popping the p. "I'm single." I stare at the top of her head. I'll look at her when I say this next part, even if she can't meet my gaze. "I don't want to be, though. And I've never had any children, but I would love to have a family of my own."

Her smile wilts, her eyes dropping down to her belly. I immediately realize how that could be construed.

"I know you don't know me well, but I was a foster kid. I work with them a lot with the Saint Foundation. I rescue animals who are alone in this world. I'm not afraid of blending blood, Tinsley. Love is love, and family is family. No matter *where* or *how*," I emphasize the words, "it came to be."

Her eyes find mine—blurry again. This time, I can tell she's not sad. Her lip twitches before she murmurs, "Christmas miracle, indeed."

*Damn fucking right.*

# Chapter Nine

## TINSLEY SNOW

My boobs hurt. My back hurts. My hair is greasy because I didn't have the energy to wash it in the shower this morning. I'm exhausted. Probably because Pix kept me up half of the night, kicking my organs and dancing on my bladder.

But...it's Thanksgiving.

I have a job. A place to call my own, *for now*. Somewhere to sleep, that's not my car. Friends.

And...wonderful coworkers. Yes. We'll go with that.

So, all and all, I'm calling these new life changes a win.

Stepping through the sliding glass hospital doors, my eyes widen as I take in the massive, modern amenities and design. This isn't at all what I was expecting from a small town like Jackson. Granted, Gresham General is on the outskirts of town, closer to the city. Still—it's beautiful here.

"Nice, huh?" Xavier quips, making me jump. My head snaps in his direction, finding his eyes trained on the same place mine had just been. I follow his gaze, taking in what must be a three or four-story vaulted ceiling. There are fancy glass art pieces suspended from the metal beams that reflect the light coming in from the floor-to-ceiling windows. It creates a mosaic of rainbows that dance through the grand space. Beautiful isn't a good enough word to describe it. It's awe-inspiring.

"Yeah," I breathe, nodding dumbly. Xavier chuckles, shaking his head.

"Mr. Saint has a knack for design." My eyes narrow on the floor, unsure how to respond to that. I want to ask questions, but I don't want anyone,

Xavier, a fellow Wonderland employee included, to know how deep my recent obsession with our boss goes. Instead, I tug on my elf skirt awkwardly. "He donates a lot of money to Gresham General, as well as other facilities in Wyoming. In exchange, they tend to give him some liberties."

He starts walking again, following our group toward the second floor, where the children's wing is. I trudge along after him, trying not to pant heavily or bombard him with more questions. The elevator ride is quick, and then suddenly, we're there...and so is *he*.

Nicolai Saint—in a Santa suit. Surrounded by seven dogs dressed as reindeer. But that's not what my eyes are locked on. My feet have barely hit the tile floor when I freeze in place. My heart begins to race wildly in my chest at the site of Nico.

He's bent down, a wide smile on his too-handsome face that I can just barely make out beneath the thick white beard he's wearing. A little boy with a cleanly shaven head, wearing a mask, is laughing hysterically as Nico tells him something with a conspiratorial whisper. Another child, a little girl no older than four, is sitting in the pile of dogs, who are licking her face sweetly and surprisingly being careful to avoid her pink arm cast.

One of the dogs, a Saint Bernard whose costume is stretched to its limits, bounds over to another child, a young teenager that's standing off to the side with a longing expression on his face. The dog knocks the child to the ground, and it feels like a weighted silence fills the air. No one moves or breathes, the dog included, as we wait to see if the boy is okay. Then, he's laughing and rolling around on the shiny white floor with the furry beast, smiling so wide he has tears in his eyes. Tears that are reflected in my own eyes as I laugh more freely than I have in ages.

I can't help but want to see Nico. His expression. His reaction. I want to see everything. The way he takes in the scene before him. The kids. The dogs. Except, when I look over at him, he's not looking at the boy or the children. He's not even paying attention to the tiny Pomeranian that's chewing on his white fur-trimmed pants.

He's looking at me.

Our eyes lock, and so much passes between us. His eyes rake down my body in a way that instantly has me squeezing my thighs together. I don't feel uncomfortable when Nico checks me out. And he does, I've realized. Especially yesterday at work. He checks me out...a lot. But it's not creepy.

It doesn't leave me feeling like my skin is coated in slime. It makes me feel *needy*.

His gaze stops on my belly, and his eyes soften. Just like with the teenage boy, there's a look of immense longing in Nico's stare. But it's more intense. It burns, setting my body on fire. His jaw ticks. His hands flex. He's restraining himself. And then, he sweeps his eyes up my body once more, settling on my face, my hair, my cheeks, and my eyes. The world stops when I see it. The way he wants me. The way he *needs me*.

My palms sweat as the intense desire to go to him fills me. He slowly pushes to his feet, feeling the same exact way I am. I take a step. He smiles. I smile back.

The room spins, and then everything goes black.

"Tanya, I don't care if you think she's fine. We aren't leaving here until you do a full check-up on her," a deep masculine voice growls. It sends a shiver down my spine, and a beeping sound quickens. "What is that? What's wrong with her?"

I hear a heavy feminine sigh, and my lip twitches. I feel exhausted and comfortable like I could nap for a day. But I'm also anxious and confused. What happened? I do a mental and physical check, making sure nothing hurts. I feel completely normal. My bump feels perfect. As if to agree, Pixie swishes and flips. I nearly groan. She's fine. So...what the hell happened?

"Nicolai," the woman tuts. Nico? Oh shit. Everything comes back in an instant, and I'm immediately mortified. I fainted. In front of him. When we were having a moment. Crap. "She's fine. The heart rate monitor is doing its job. We're observing her, and so far, everything looks perfect."

"Clearly, that's not the case," he snaps. My brows furrow. I know I should open my eyes, but for some reason, I don't want to. My hands flex, and that's when I feel it. He's holding my hand. Yeah. Definitely not waking up. Not yet. "She fainted, Tanya. I don't care if you're the best doctor in the Midwest. You're obviously missing something."

"Jesus, save me," she mutters, sounding exasperated. I like her. "Did she hit her stomach when she fell?"

There's a heavy pause. "No," he murmurs, sounding dejected. "I caught her the second I knew she was falling."

"Okay, then. She likely just had a vasovagal syncope episode." I can hear his gasp, and my lip twitches again. He's kind of cute when he's freaking out. "Before you start yelling again, it's completely normal at this stage of pregnancy. She will be completely fine after she rests a bit."

"And the baby?" His voice is a hushed rasp that instantly goes straight to my heart. "Is the baby okay?"

Another pause. "Are you the father, Nico?"

"Yes," he says, his thumb running across the back of my hand soothingly. My chest squeezes painfully. The heart rate monitor begins to go wild again. "If that's what you need to hear for you to tell me how the baby is, then yes." And my heart sinks. At this point, I'm pretty thankful I'm already lying down.

The doctor clicks her tongue in disapproval. "Unfortunately, that doesn't count in this situation, no matter how powerful you are."

Nico makes a pained sound. "Look," he murmurs. "She's my employee. She fainted on the job in my arms." He exhales roughly, his voice dropping. "More than that, I care about her. A lot. And the baby. Just tell me the baby is okay, so I can leave you alone."

Something shifts on my stomach, and I immediately know it's the fetal monitor. I wait with bated breath for the whooshing sound of Pixie's heart. The sound I've grown to love so much. It takes a moment, but then, it's there, filling the room. I inhale deeply, absorbing the perfect sound. I'm so tuned into listening to Pixie that I almost miss it. The sharp breath. The way his hand squeezes mine roughly.

"That's the baby, isn't it?" he whispers, his voice way more emotional than I expect it to be. "The baby's heartbeat."

"Beautiful, huh?" the doctor sighs happily. "One of my favorite sounds ev—"

"Shh," Nico hushes her. The doctor chuckles. They fall into a content silence as he listens to Pixie. I do the same, unable to help myself. "Can you leave it on her for a while?"

I swear I hear her groan. "She really doesn't need to be observed any longer, Nicolai. Tinsley is okay. The baby is perfect. They can go home."

Silence meets her declaration, this one the heaviest yet. I don't know why, but Nico grows tense next to me. I can't see him, but I can *feel* him. When he finally speaks, his voice has hardened a bit. "Does she need to be on bed rest? Should she stop working? Does she need someone to look after her and the baby to make sure it doesn't happen again?"

"Hmm," she mumbles. "Does Tinsley have difficult duties at work? Standing for long periods? Lifting heavy items?"

"We gave her a chair, but the stubborn woman refuses to use the damn thing," he grumbles, sounding like a petulant child. "She doesn't have to lift things, but we do have long, busy days. I don't—" he breaks off. For some reason, I can just picture him raking his hand through his hair with the hand not wrapped around mine. "I know she won't stop working. Tinsley is independent. She wants to provide for Pixie. But I'll give her the option to take a leave if she wants it." My breath catches, and my stomach flips at the way he somehow knows me so well. "What about being alone? Is this going to keep happening?"

"There's no way to know. The fainting itself isn't an issue. But if she falls or hits her head or belly, that's where it becomes a problem. Does she live alone?"

"Yes," he rasps. "But not for long."

My eyes finally snap open at that. The doctor gives me a sly, knowing look. Nico doesn't notice I'm awake. His gaze is locked on the monitor displaying mine and Pixie's heartbeats. I swear, if

I didn't know any better, I'd say there are hearts in his eyes. He's lost his Santa hat and beard, but the suit and stuffing are still in place. My eyes quickly scan the room, finding us in a large, private suite that I'm pretty sure is on the birthing floor. Poor guy must have thought I was in labor. There's something incredibly sweet about his over-the-top, protective reaction. How many times did I long for this? Dream about it? Pixie's dad sharing this experience with us.

Too many to count.

"Oh, yeah?" the doctor chuckles. "Does she know that?"

Nico grimaces, running his free hand through his thick stubble. "I want her to stay with me," he murmurs. The maddening circles he's rubbing on the back of my hand never stop, and it does something to soothe the panic coursing through me. "My house is big enough. I live alone. I could hire a nanny, or nurse, or whatever she needs to make her feel comfortable." He swallows thickly, and I track the way his adam's apple bobs. "I just don't want her to be alone or scared. She's been through enough."

And there go the waterworks. The doctor notices my tears and gives me a sympathetic look before patting my other hand. She glances back at Nico. "You're a good man, Nicolai Saint. One of the best out there. I have every confidence in you doing what's right. If Tinsley agrees to stay with you *or* someone else, it's probably for the best, for now." I feel the weight of her words. The way she's no doubt speaking them for me. She cocks her head to the side, eyes narrowing. "Just ensure you're respectful of the poor girl, or I'll have your ass."

With that, she spins on her heel, leaving the two of us alone. Before she exits, she calls over her shoulder, "Ten more minutes. Then I'm discharging her. She's fine, Nico. They both are. You did good."

The door clicks and Nico releases a heaving breath, his body seeming to crumple. I watch his profile, silent tears still streaming down my face as my emotions catch up with me.

He wants me to move in with him? To take care of not just me but Pixie? I swallow silently, my eyes burning hot. We may have just met, but I'd be stupid to ignore the pull between us. Does that mean I think I'm ready to jump into anything? I don't know. Is that even what he wants? By the way he was talking, I'd say yes.

That should terrify me. It should make me run for the hills, especially after everything I've been through. But Nico is different. I know that's a naive thing to say, but I know it down to my soul. To my bones. The way he looks at me, at my belly...he cares. Vincent never looked at me that way. He never even noticed I was a person, just a body to use.

I squeeze my eyes shut. I try not to think of him, but sometimes, it's hard. Pixie has already had such a rough life, and she hasn't even been born yet. I want better for her. So badly, I want her to have a family. A good life. I want to be safe and protected. I want her to have what I never had. *Love.* I know I can give her that on my own, but—Lottie's words ring clear in my head, echoed by Nico's.

*You don't have to do this alone if you don't want to. Everything you've ever wanted is right in front of you. You just have to be brave enough to take it.*

"I'm so fucking sorry, Tinsley," Nico whispers. I feel him drop to a crouch next to me before his forehead hits the back of our joined hands. My eyes peel open to watch him. I can't see his face, but I can tell he's devastated. I just don't understand why, and I suddenly have the overwhelming need to comfort him.

"I'm sorry your life has been so hard. I'm sorry Pixie didn't get the start in life she deserved. I'm sorry that you felt so unsafe that you had to run. I know what that feels like. I know what being cold and hungry is like, and it breaks my heart that you had to go through that." He releases a heavy breath, and I barely choke down a sob. I don't understand any of this. I don't understand why he...*we* feel so much so soon...but we do.

*I do.*

"I promise you never have to be alone again if you don't want to. It's reckless. Fast. Insane." He groans, shaking his head. His soft skin swishes against mine. "I know I'm too fucking old for you. I'm double your age. It's crazy." He gulps. "But it doesn't change this wild need to be with you. To protect you and Pixie. I just need you to let me take care of you."

My lips part, releasing a puff of air along with one nearly silent word. *"Yes."*

# Chapter Ten

## TINSLEY SNOW

H<small>IS HEAD SNAPS UP</small>, his wide, red eyes meeting mine. The monitor goes nuts, but I'd expect nothing different. I just agreed to move in with a stranger. Yet, I can't find a single nerve or thought inside of me that wants to take it back.

He stands slowly, leaning over me, our faces mere inches apart. "Say it again."

I swallow and bat my tears away. "I'll move in with you." I tug my lip between my teeth and bite down against the swell of emotions. "I'll let you take care of..." I break off before choking out, "Us."

Terrifying. This should be terrifying. But—it's not. It's right. So damn right.

Nico smiles so wide that his dimples pop out beneath his short beard. Dimples I've grown to love in just a few short days. Ones I've grown addicted to. "Can I kiss you, Tinsley Snow?"

I don't question what my gut wants. I don't think twice. I just nod.

And then, Nicolai Saint's lips are on mine. I gasp the second I feel the soft press of his mouth. The kiss is slow and sweet. A joining of two broken, lonely people who've found a kinship in a stranger. It's not my first kiss, but it might as well be with the way it takes my breath away.

Nico slides his tongue along the seam of my mouth, and I immediately open for him. He groans, palming my cheeks to direct me where he wants me. I let him. I sink into him. The kiss. His mouth and taste. So good. Sweet and savory, like milk and cookies. I smile against his lips. He pulls away, resting his forehead on mine. We're both slightly out of breath as our eyes lock. His lip tips up.

"What's so funny, pretty girl?" he murmurs. I sigh, shaking my head. I can feel how hot my cheeks are from blushing. He chuckles before sobering. "Are you sure? I don't want to rush you or push you into anything. I just want you to be safe and comf—"

I reach up, tugging his lips back down to mine. Nico shudders, responding without skipping a beat. This kiss is different. More intense as it quickly heats. I feel how wet I am from just the pass of his tongue and his scent. The feeling of him against me. I moan, tugging his lip between my teeth as my motions grow frantic. Need swells within me. An ache builds so fast and strong that all other thoughts fly out the window.

"Nico," I pant. "Please."

He groans, tugging my mouth closer to his. He's just as frantic. His desire just as strong. He shifts, and his cock presses against my hand on the bed. I gasp when I feel how hard and big he is. My fingers immediately wrap around him, squeezing roughly. He releases a choking sound, but I don't release him. I need him. Need him now. The desire that's been building my entire pregnancy, thanks to my wild hormones, is at a breaking point. More than that, it's *him*. I need *him*.

Nico's hips thrust into my palm, his tongue diving into my mouth to lick and explore every inch of me. He grinds, panting and moaning against me. My thighs rub together to the point that I'm seconds from cumming without even being touched. I'm soaked. Completely drenched. My breasts are heaving, aching with need. My nipples pulse and throb before turning wet. Shit. I'm leaking. I should care, but I can't find it in me right now. Not when I'm so close to the edge.

I pull away, locking eyes with his. "Nico, please," I gasp out. My thighs are now actively rubbing beneath the sheet. Everything is sensitive. So sensitive.

"What do you need, baby?" he rasps, his voice thick. "Do you need to cum on my fingers?" I nod, breathing harshly. He groans but wastes no time. His hand slides under the sheet, my knee-length skirt, and up to the apex of my thighs. I drop my knees open. The first pass of his knuckle over my panties has my hips thrusting up. He groans again before shoving them to the side and swiping over my sensitive flesh. "Fuck, Tinsley. This all for me?"

I nod again. Nico's jaw ticks. He flicks my clit, and I groan. "Say it," he murmurs. "Tell me who has this pretty little pussy dripping all over the bed right now."

I suck in a breath at his command. "You, Nico," I breathe. He flicks my clit again, and I nearly scream in pleasure.

"I think I like Mr. Saint better when my fingers are coated in your sloppy cunt juices." I shiver at his crass words, and he chuckles darkly. "Give me what I want, and I'll make this pussy squirt."

"Fuck," I gasp, shakily jacking his cock and thrusting my hips up. "Please, Mr. Saint. Please make me cum."

He squeezes his eyes shut, seeming to control himself. He flicks his gaze open and peels my fingers from his dick. My eyes widen. "It's not for me, baby. Not this time. I'm not cumming again until I can stuff your sweet pussy with my seed." He presses down on my clit hard just as the words leave his lips. I detonate, crying out before remembering where we are. I go to cover my mouth, but Nico softly bats my hand away, his eyes hard as he continues to rub my pussy in quick, hard circles. "No," he growls. "Let everyone hear you. Let everyone know who's making you cum so hard you have no choice but to scream."

And I do. "Holy shit," I whimper, riding out the longest and most intense orgasm of my life. When I finally come down, Nico smiles and slowly pulls his hand from between my thighs. His fingers go straight into his mouth. His eyes flutter closed as he moans around my flavor. I whimper again. Why is that so hot?

"Perfect," he breathes. "Fucking perfect." His eyes are soft and on mine, as he says this, and I don't miss his double meaning. His gaze drops down to my chest. He gulps audibly.

I follow his gaze and groan in frustration. I'm not embarrassed that my boobs leaked. It's normal. But now, it's impossible not to see the dark spots on my nipples. "Sorry," I whisper, though I don't know why.

Nico huffs a breath and bends down. His eyes flick up to mine, watching me watch him as his tongue slowly laps at the wet spots. His moan rivals my own when I came, and I shiver at the sound. He repeats the process on the other side, licking up my mess.

"I can't wait for the day you let me suck your sweet cream from these perfect tits, baby," he murmurs. My mouth drops open in shock. Nico shrugs. "I find you so utterly sexy, Tinsley. Every inch of you. Your body, your breasts, your belly." His hands twitch again, and I know he wants to touch my stomach but is holding back. He shakes his head. "You're a goddamned goddess."

He looks down at my belly, his hand hovering. "Can I?"

I open my mouth to respond. To tell him he can touch me wherever he wants, but the door almost slamming open has my jaw snapping shut and Nico quickly standing. A male nurse walks in, snapping his gum loudly. He grins and throws me a knowing wink. "Time to get you out of here, Mrs. Saint."

My heart beats rapidly at his words and the *rightness* of them. I wait for Nico to correct the man, but he doesn't. He doesn't even twitch. Holy shit. All he does is smile down at me and murmur, "Let's get you home."

# Chapter Eleven

## nicolai saint

**M**Y PALMS ARE SWEATING profusely, matching the wet stain I can feel trickling down my back. I should have taken this damn suit off before we left the hospital. I should have done a lot of things...like not panicking at my girl's bedside like a lovesick fool. Or gotten her off the second my fingers touched her porcelain skin for the first time. I shouldn't have basically cried at the thought of something being wrong with her or the baby.

But I did. I did all of those things. And I don't regret a single moment of them. Not one.

I smile to myself as I pull into my expansive four car garage. My home is large but not gaudy. Yet, I can't help but be terrified about what Tinsley will think when she sees it. Will she freak out? Think it's too much? Will she be too afraid to touch anything? God, I hope not.

Groaning, I take a moment to compose myself before climbing out of my jeep. I swallow when I see her small Toyota Corolla pull up the long, pebbled driveway. She shouldn't be driving that tiny ass car. It's not safe in this snow. Snow chains be damned. I shake my head and sigh, already resigned to the fight we'll be having when she realizes I've bought her a new car. A safer one. Stepping forward, I direct Tinsley to pull into the space next to mine in the garage. Her eyes are wide, and as I assumed, there's a blanket of fear coating her features.

Well, shit.

After leaving the hospital, I followed Tinsley to the office she's been staying at to help her pack up her meager belongings. Something else I've already rectified. One of the many surprises I have in store for her here. She insisted on bringing her own car. Something I initially fought but understood. She needs the safety of having an escape. After picking up a to-go order from Lottie's, she followed me here...to our home.

Now, I just need to get her out of the car. Something I feel might be a tad difficult, judging by the way she's gripping her steering wheel. I smile. She has no idea what's in store for her.

Closing the distance between us, I knock softly on the window. She jumps and shakes her head. I watch her as she gives herself a muttered pep talk, making me chuckle. She nods once and throws the door open, hitting me in the gut as she goes. I double over, gasping for breath.

"Oh, shit," she cries, patting me all over as if to check for blood. "Shit, Nico. I'm so sorry. I was just freaking out. I don't know why. Well, that's not true. I know why. This is just all so fast and crazy. Your house is huge. Like really huge. Beautiful though, but huge." I smirk, standing to my full height as I watch her flail about like a wet kitten. She's so lost in her rambling; she hasn't even noticed I'm fine. "You live in a lumberjack's version of Cinderella's castle. Did you see that driveway? I was on it for like five minutes straight, I swear. And the—"

Unable to take her adorable antics any longer, I dive forward, shutting her up with a rough kiss that's borderline punishing. Tinsley gasps into my mouth as I cuff the back of her neck, dragging her closer, needing her deeper. I want Tinsley Snow so deep inside of me that there is no telling where she ends and I begin. She melts into me, her arms going limp at her sides. I slow my pace and lessen my pressure until our lips are nearly just resting on one another's. We breathe each other in. The tension leaves her body. She shudders. I grin. She slaps my padded stomach with the back of her hand. I laugh.

This. This is what it's supposed to be like. And this is exactly why I know we'll work out. There's an ease between the two of us. One that usually comes with time. But it's here, and I'm not giving it up.

I drop my hold on her but keep my hands on her shoulders until I know she's steady. She blinks up at me, looking dazed as hell. "Wow," she breathes, her fingers tracing her lips.

I cock a brow. "Good?" She nods before finally giving me that huge smile I adore so much. I grip her hand, guiding her through the garage and into my house. Tinsley gasps. My chest squeezes as nerves prick over my skin. "I hope you like it."

*Nice, Nico. Really fucking eloquent.*

She tugs on my hand, and I release her, content to lean against the island in the kitchen we'd just entered as I watch her take in everything. Tinsley explores, running her fingers over the couch and the walls. She reaches the center of the large open-concept room and spins in a circle. Her long, white, blonde hair is in two thick braids beneath her elf cap, landing just below her full breasts. Breasts that are pushing against the thin material of her green, velvet costume. Her skirt lifts on a breeze as she spins, showing off the creamy patch of skin above her socks and below her skirt. I groan, adjusting my cock that hasn't stopped throbbing since I met her. In the last week, I've jacked off...a lot. But I meant what I told her today. After having my hands on Tinsley's body, I won't be cumming again until it's inside her slick pussy. The insatiable need to mark her, claim her, has become all-consuming.

"It's incredible, Nico," she breathes, sounding slightly winded. "Really, it's beautiful."

"Not as beautiful as you," I say, meaning it completely. Tinsley blushes. I smirk, meeting her between the kitchen and living room. I palm her cheeks, unable to stop touching her. "I know it's fast, but I meant what I said, Tinsley. I want you. We can take this however slow you need, but just know I'm here." I glance down at her belly. "I want you both."

"Nico," she whispers. I hear her swallow thickly before picking up my hand. My eyes flick to hers, shocked and confused, even though I know what she's about to do. *I hope.*

My heart races as Tinsley brings my palm up to her belly. The beautiful belly that has enraptured me from day one. She's stunning, pregnant, and swollen. Growing a human inside of her. Utterly captivating. But also, goddamned if the sight of her like this doesn't turn me on to the point of pain. She presses our combined hands down on the underside of her stomach. Her bump is softer than I was expecting. But still... there's nothing else like it. Nothing. I never got to experience this with my ex-wife. Never got to create a family. I wanted to. God, I wanted a family so badly. But now, here at this moment, I know why it never worked out for us. Life had other plans for me. Better plans.

She shifts my hand to the side. I stand stock still, waiting for the movement I know I should feel. I hold my breath, but it never comes. I glance up at Tinsley, and she offers me a sad, soft look. "She's sleeping."

"Are you sure?" I murmur, my forehead pinched. "Are you sure she's okay?"

Tinsley chuckles, releasing my hand. I don't want to let go, but reluctantly, I do, knowing this was already a big step for us. "Yes. I'm positive. You heard her heart. She's—"

"Perfect," I say, nodding. "She's perfect. Just like her mama."

She sucks in a breath. "You have to stop saying things like that."

I shake my head, gripping her hand to lead her upstairs. "Not a fucking chance, Goddess."

She sucks in a breath at the nickname but tries to cover it up with a scoff as she follows along after me. "Did you design this yourself?" she asks, referring to the house just as we hit the bottom level of the stairs.

Turning back, I smile down at her and shrug. "Yes, and no. I hired a really popular home designer from Colorado called Huxley Homes. They specialize in this kind of thing. They mill the pine from the forest surrounding their personal properties and frequently replant to keep the forest in control. They have a knack for homes of all sizes that work well with the land instead of against it."

"Cabin-chic," she huffs. "It's a cabin-mansion."

I chuckle. I guess you could say that. Coming in at just under 4,000 sq ft, two levels, plus the underground four-car garage, it does sound sprawling. But it's cozy. We reach the top floor where all the bedrooms are, and I turn to her.

"I wanted something that felt warm." Suddenly, I feel twitchy. Palming the back of my head, I look down, finding my black Santa boots suddenly interesting. "This house feels warm to me. The fireplaces and wood. The natural stone." I tip my shoulder. "I grew up in a trailer in a shitty neighborhood. My parents were good people, but we were poor. Yet, I was happy. I never longed for more. Never felt cold." I meet her eyes, something passing between us. "Until I did."

She nods knowingly, reaching out to squeeze my hand. "So, you made sure you'd always feel warm. Safe. I get it." She rubs her thumb across my skin, and I shiver. "It's truly beautiful, Nico. I love it."

I exhale a breath I hadn't realized I'd been holding and grin at her. "Wait till you see this next part."

I tug her along, a bit more pep to my step now that I know she's not panicking over the house. Hopefully, this doesn't send her over the edge. I'm not going to show her all the things I did for her. Not yet...but there is one thing I know she'll love. I push the door open to the room right next to mine. I gave her the master, changing the décor slightly to make it warmer than its previous white walls. I wanted her to have the space, the largest bathroom, and closet. But, more than that, this room has an attached nursery. One that's newly renovated. Something Logan Huxley, the owner of the design company I hired, apparently has in his own home. At first, I wasn't sold on the idea. But now I know it was the right choice.

Still, that's not what I'm excited about.

Tinsley screeches, diving forward. I barely have time to catch her before she collides with the floor. I wrap my arms around her gently and lower her to the floor with a hiss.

"Be careful," I grunt. Unfortunately, my reprimand is lost beneath a loud sniffle and coo as she squeezes her cat Stella half to death. I chuckle. I pat her head softly, then glower at the elf hat. "Don't choke the poor beast, baby," I chide as I set about removing the clips keeping her hat in place.

Tinsley barely notices my actions, but that's fine. Once I've gotten it removed, I take everything to the bathroom and set it on the counter. I flick my gaze over to her once more, finding her rocking the cat back and forth. Leaning against the doorway, I cross my arms over my chest and just watch her. I can't deny the overwhelming rightness at having Tinsley here, in my space, in my room. Soon, in my bed. I might not sleep with her, not yet, but I may or may not have left my own sheets intact, knowing they'd smell like me.

Tinsley looks up at me, her face blotchy and pink. "How?"

I smile, scuffing my boot on the floor. "Yesterday, I went to your old apartment and spoke to your neighbor. Apparently, she was more than happy to give the little demon back." I glower at the beast, the scratches running up and down my arms burning as I do. The fluffy creature hisses, and I swear she sounds satanic. "I knew you'd want her back if you had a safe place to have her." I shrug. "Now you do."

"Nicolai," she breathes, sending goosebumps down my spine. I like the sound of my name on her lips like that. She shakes her head before giggling softly. "Christmas fucking miracle."

She keeps saying that, and I know to her, it has some sort of important meaning. But the truth is, I'm not a Christmas anything. The true miracle is Tinsley. I push off the wall and make my way to her, helping her from the floor.

"Do you want to see the rest of the house now or eat and take a bath?" I murmur, my hands sliding up and down her arms. She groans, her eyes fluttering closed, and I know my girl is exhausted. "Maybe food while you bathe?" I suggest, only partially kidding.

Her eyes blink open, her head tilting to the side with a mischievous glint. "What about you? It's Thanksgiving. I don't want you to eat alone." She tugs her lip between her teeth. "Maybe we can do both. Together." My cock throbs at her insinuation. I swallow down a groan and shake my head, squeezing her biceps.

"Soon, Goddess." I press a lingering kiss to her forehead before dipping down to her ear. "Soon, I'll have you splayed out before me like the feast you are." She shudders. "But not yet. I may have you in my home already, Tinsley Snow, but I want to do this right. You deserve that." I press my hand to her belly, cupping it tenderly. "You both do."

# Chapter Twelve

## TINSLEY SNOW

"Good morning," Nico greets, a bright smile on his handsome face. I stumble as I enter the kitchen, nearly choking on my tongue at the sight of him.

"Uhh," I murmur, my brows dipping as my eyes slide over to the clock above the stone fireplace. "It's only 6:00 am. Why are you—" I break off, gesturing to his overall appearance. Black slacks, a red button-down, shiny black shoes, and...I cock my head to the side. "Is that a candy cane tie?"

Nico barks out a laugh, turning back to the stove. "Come sit down, Tinsley."

He juts his chin at the kitchen table, which is surprisingly low-key considering how fancy everything else in this sprawling house looks. Well, actually, that's not true. Though his house *is* massive, it's simple and homey. A fact that he proved when he gave me a tour last night that I partially slept through but was eager to have. He showed me all seven bedrooms, including an eighth downstairs, solely dedicated to his dogs and now Stella. He also gave me a ten-minute lecture on how pregnant women aren't allowed near cat poo. Yes. You heard me—cat poo.

I nod absently and drop down into the chair, tugging my fleece robe tighter over my belly. It's a struggle, but I make it work.

"Is there a dress code for breakfast or something?" I mumble, my mouth salivating as I watch him pour a cup of coffee. I'm seconds from begging for a cup of the sweet nectar when Nico moves to the fridge and pulls out a bottle of sugar-free, non-fat whipped cream. He covers the top of the coffee in the creamy goodness and then sprinkles it with a light dusting of peppermint sprinkles.

He deposits the concoction in front of me with an awkward, almost nervous look. "Lottie said you can have decaf once a day." He shifts back on his heels. "I didn't believe her, so I called Dr. Talbot, and she agreed."

Instantly I want to cry. God, he's so damn perfect. At this rate, I won't be able to stop my heart from falling for him. Not that I'd want to. "Thank you," I whisper, my voice a little more choked up than I'd like.

*Get it together, Tinsley. It's just coffee.*

"And no," he chuckles. "I've just been up for an hour or so. I run in the mornings, and I have to go into the office today."

I blow on the piping hot coffee, considering that. "Is that for the foundation?"

Nico shakes his head, dropping butter into a sizzling pan. He shoots me a look, his eyes softening. "Do you want to know a secret?" His voice is barely above a whisper, as though someone else is in the house and might overhear.

I lean in, nodding rapidly. Nico chuckles, turning back to the pan. He whisks a thick white batter a few times before pouring some of it into the skillet. "I own every Wonderland across the Midwest."

"I know," I murmur, feeling a wave of insecurity wash over me as my mind computes how much money that equates.

Nico looks over his shoulder at me, his brow cocking. "But did you know I'm stepping down as CEO to focus on the Saint Foundation?"

I gasp, my hand clutching my throat as though I've got a pair of invisible pearls there. "Seriously?" Nico nods. "But—" I'm practically stuttering. "But why?"

His smile drops, and his jaw begins to tick before he focuses back on the food. "I didn't start Wonderland alone, and I didn't start it to get rich."

"I know," I say, knowing without a shadow of a doubt. Nico doesn't seem like that kind of person. He sighs, his head dropping slightly as he braces his hands on either side of the stove and squeezes the counter.

"You don't, though, Tinsley. I may not have started Wonderland for the money, but I did lose myself to it once." His forearms flex. "I was married before. Not for long, but it was a long time ago." I tuck my lips between my teeth to hold in my reaction. I'm not so naïve to think that Nico didn't have a life before me. I know how old he is—but married?

"What happened?" I'm almost afraid to ask. Worried it'll dampen the way I see him now. Perfect. He's perfect.

He flips the pancake and starts a second batch of batter. "I was too consumed with Wonderland Corporation. With building it. With the money." He tuts. "Don't get me wrong. My ex and I were never meant to last for the long haul. We didn't mesh." He glances at me. "We didn't just *fit*, you know?" I nod, knowing now more than ever what he means. "But I still failed as a husband. I wasn't there for her like I should have been." Turning back to take the pancake off the stove and add more butter, he continues. "She's happier now. Way happier. But somewhere along the line, I realized that I wanted more. I got so caught up in building a life that I forgot to live it. I won't make that mistake again. Especially not now."

My mouth gapes open. Once again, I'm stumbling over my words. "Are you saying you're giving up your position—" I break off, swallowing thickly as my hands clam up. "For me?"

Nico clears his throat, shifting awkwardly on his feet, his back still to me. "No." For some reason, my heart sinks. It has no right to. Absolutely no right. But it does. "Not at first."

"What does that mean, Nico?" I murmur.

He finally turns to face me, leaning against the counter with his beautiful forearms crossed over his chest. "It means that I knew before I met you that I'd be stepping down. I started the process months ago." He runs a hand through his hair. "But, after I met you, I knew down to my bones that it was the right choice. I said it yesterday at the hospital. I know this is fast, but I don't care. I'm not getting any younger, and Pixie will be here before we know it. I want this, Tinsley. You," he gestures to my belly. "Her." Nico tugs his lip between his teeth, biting down hard as his eyes turn heated. "A whole bunch more."

"You—" I whisper-gasp. "You want more babies with me?"

He nods, blatantly adjusting his very hard cock that's tenting his slacks. "A lot of them."

With that, he turns back and finishes working on a short stack of pancakes. Meanwhile, I'm still gaping as my mind tries to process all of that.

When he finally speaks again, he changes the subject completely, offering me a much-needed reprieve. "How did you sleep? Was the bed okay? Did you find everything in the bathroom last night?"

Right. Last night, when he drew me a lukewarm bath in the massive, deep soaking tub before filling it with sugar cookie-scented bubbles. The bath that I *so* wanted to beg him to join me in. Before I had the chance, Nico smiled, kissed my forehead, and told me goodnight, leaving me in the middle of the room, gaping after him.

"The bath was wonderful." I swallow down a mouthful of coffee, releasing a contented sigh. "The bed was even better."

Is it weird to tell him that it smelled like him? Like juniper and balsam with a touch of cinnamon? Like Christmas. Like *home*. Yeah. Definitely don't do that, Tinsley. Do not tell the man he smells like home and that you rubbed yourself all over his sheets before getting yourself off…repeatedly.

I clear my throat, my clit throbbing in time with my heartbeat as I watch Nico flip pancakes. His sleeves are rolled up, exposing his veiny forearms that are dusted with dark hair. They flex with his movements, and it does nothing to calm the reaction my body is having right now. I relax back in my chair, content to enjoy the show. My eyes flit between Nico, my coffee, his house, and the sprawling view out of the massive windows. The backyard is covered in a fine layer of snow. His house is backed up to a large mountain, dotted with pine trees. Everything here is beautiful. Peaceful. I love it.

Visions of Pixie and her siblings running through the yard fill my mind so suddenly and viscerally that I drop the coffee mug. Hot liquid sloshes over the side, and I panic. "Shit," I screech, jumping to my feet to find a towel or washcloth, but Nico is there before I can even move.

He calmly picks up my hands, wiping the coffee from my skin that I hadn't even noticed. He presses down on my shoulder, guiding me to sit before cleaning up the table and cup. He says nothing. Doesn't yell about me staining his fancy oak table. Doesn't freak out. He just takes care of me and the problem as though it's no big deal. That shouldn't punch me right in the gut, but it does because those visions I'd had before immediately come rolling back in. He'd be such a good father. He's kind. Loving. Patient. He cares about people that he doesn't need to care about simply because his heart is *that* big. All of the things everyone around town has said about Nicolai Saint, again and again, are completely and utterly *accurate*.

In a way it has no right to, everything becomes crystal clear. Nico moves to step back to the stove, but I grip his hand, turning him back to me. His eyes are soft, but his brow is furrowed, like he's worried. His gaze dips down to my belly as if to check on Pixie, something he constantly does, and I know this decision is the right one.

"I want to try," I say, my voice calm and sure. "With you. I want to try this out. Us."

He drops to his knees, his hands palming my cheeks. "Yeah?"

I nod, feeling uncharacteristically giddy. "Yeah."

He releases a tortured-sounding breath and presses his lips to mine. He immediately sinks into me; morning breath be damned. Before I can lose myself in the kiss, Nico pulls away. His grin is just as wide as mine as he bends down and kisses my belly. "Good morning, Pixie girl."

That's the exact moment I fall for Nicolai Saint.

*I'm so screwed.*

# Chapter Thirteen

## TINSLEY SNOW

A WEEK PASSES IN the blink of an eye. Things stay the same but don't.

Nico and I wake up early. He makes breakfast and decaf coffee. We chat about everything and nothing. He kisses me stupid. We go to work together. Sometimes he comes with me. Other times, he goes to the Wonderland Co. building, which I've learned is about an hour away in the city. Every day though, he picks me up when I'm off. He pats me down and kisses me until

I'm breathless before dropping to his knees and kissing my bump. Then, he has a twenty-minute minimum conversation with Candy about how I did that day. Whether or not I sat down and kept my duties restricted as the doctor suggested. If I acted normally or had any dizzy spells. If I ate enough. And so on and so on.

After that, he takes me home and makes me dinner. Sometimes, we watch a movie. I inevitably fall asleep every time with Nico rubbing my back. He's surprisingly great at it. He carries me upstairs and tucks me into bed, making sure I'm settled for the night and Pixie's okay, before pulling himself from my room. Every night, I see him struggle with himself as he leaves. I know he wants to stay. I know he wants to fall asleep wrapped around me. *I want that*...and so much more. Then, the next day, the process repeats.

At first, it was overwhelming.

Now, it's everything.

I look forward to his overprotective ways and his somewhat neurotic anxiety over Pixie and me. I love it...probably too much. The problem with being a person who was never shown an ounce of kindness in their life, especially their childhood, is they're more likely to cling to the first person who gives it to them. I'm aware of that.

It's one of the reasons the court pegged me the way they did during the trial. Sad little trailer park girl with a broken family and abusive dad. They even brought in a psychologist, no doubt paid off by that *man*, to attest to my mental instability. Regardless, it's something I'm aware of and trying to be mindful of as Nico and I move forward. I don't want to cling to him just because he's kind to me and offering me a safe place to rest my head. I want to choose him because it's right.

And so far, nothing has proven that any different.

He further made this clear by offering to come with me to my doctor's appointment today. No, not just offered…insisted. Now, here we sit in a pink and blue office filled with photos of babies, a pregnant woman in every other chair. I'd expect him to be panicking. Making a run for it. But he's not. If anything, he's more excited than I am. He's practically dancing in his chair.

I grip his thigh when a heavily pregnant woman shoots him an annoyed look for the third time. "Calm down, babe," I murmur. Nico's eyes snap to mine, heated and wild at the nickname slip. It's happened before, and I think we both know it's not a slip. More of a slow integration into this relationship on my part. "Are you nervous?"

His brows dip. Nico blankets my hand with his, weaving our fingers together. "Yes." He sucks his lip between his teeth, his eyes raking down my body. He shifts in his chair. "But not for the reason you think." He leans in, his lips and stubble brushing over my ear in a way that has me shivering. "I'm worried that the second I see her moving inside of you, I'll drop to my knees and propose." I suck in a sharp breath. His hand moves to my thigh, slowly traveling up, up, up. I smack mine on top, halting his progress. He chuckles. "And I'm nervous I'll get painfully hard in the middle of this appointment thinking about all the ways I want to fuck you. How badly I want to fill you so full of my cum, you'll be pregnant again the second it's possible." I'm trembling now. My eyes flutter closed. "But mostly, Tinsley—" He breaks off, swallowing thickly. "I'm nervous about how seeing Pixie in her mama's belly is going to make me fall more in love with you."

I gasp. My eyes snap open, and I rear back, shocked at what he just said. Surely, he didn't mean that. Not in that way. My mouth opens before snapping shut again. I'm entirely at a loss for words. But the look on Nico's face tells me that wasn't a mistake or a slip of the tongue. No…he meant that.

"H—" I barely get a puff of breath out before a woman steps through the door, calling me back. Nico chuckles at my dumbfounded expression and helps me stand before ushering me to the exam room. I completely blanked out while they took my vitals and got me situated on the exam table. I'm still in shock when the doctor finally joins us.

Dr. Talbot smiles widely when she sees Nico at my side, his large hands wrapped around mine. But she doesn't look surprised. "Tinsley," she greets before nodding respectfully at the man next to me. "Nicolai."

Nico dips his head but doesn't stand to shake her hand. If anything, he squeezes mine harder. "Tanya. Nice to see you again."

She tuts, rolling her eyes as she drops down onto her stool. "Let's cut the bullshit." I bark out a laugh at her bluntness but instantly relax at the informality. "I see you've wormed your way into sweet Tinsley's life." She snaps on her gloves, tilting her head to the side. "But have you earned your way into her heart yet?"

Nico sucks in a nearly inaudible sound, clearly at a loss of how to respond. I see him struggle for words, and the sight of it's almost my undoing. I bring our joined hands to my chest and pat them with my free hand.

"Yes," I say softly with a nod. My eyes move over to Nico's, my words just for him. "He has."

He stands then, bending over my body to press his lips to mine. It's short, our company considered. When he pulls away, he mutters against my mouth, "Goddammit, Tinsley. You're going to fucking kill me here, and I haven't even seen her."

I chuckle, looking at the doctor when he sits back down. "We're ready."

She looks damn near teary-eyed as she sets about preparing the external ultrasound. She lifts my shirt, and I momentarily panic. This is the first time Nico is seeing my belly. It's one thing to say you love my body when I'm covered up in chunky sweaters and robes. But it's a whole other to see my large, pale, swollen stomach up close. I'm littered with stretch marks. And not the cute white kind some women get just near their hips. No. I look like I was electrocuted, and my belly took the brunt of the damage, leaving with deep red and purple wiggly lines, from my pelvis, nearly up to my breasts. I don't hate my marks. I know they mean I've provided for my child. Made a safe home for her to grow. But, fuck, if

I'm not self-conscious about the insane ways my body has changed.

The doctor doesn't bat an eye as she squirts the warm gel over my skin, still fiddling with the wand. But Nico… he's gone utterly still next to me. My eyes squeeze shut, not wanting to see the rejection. The realization that I'm not what he envisioned.

"Fuck," he breathes. My eyes burn. I can't look at him. Can't. Yet, I'm forced to when his hands find my cheeks, tilting my head upwards to meet his. "Perfect, baby." He leans down closer, finding my ear once more. "I'm nervous now, Tinsley. So damn nervous."

I look up at him then, finding a moment of bravery. His eyes are heated, probably reflecting exactly what I'm feeling. "Which part?" I ask, referring to our conversation in the lobby.

Nico drops back down in his chair, a shit-eating grin on his face. "All of it."

The wand is placed on my stomach, making me jump at the cold temperature. The doctor sighs heavily. "Alright, mom and dad. Are you ready?"

I shiver at the rightness in her words, and Nico practically bounces in his chair. "Fuck, yes."

It feels like it takes hours before the doctor turns the monitor in our direction, though it's likely only been minutes. She smiles, moving the wand back and forth to find things to point out. The second the image is clear, I'm crying. It's not my first time seeing Pixie. Not even my tenth. Initially, I was in and out of clinics due to my anxiety and court stuff. But it's the first time I'm seeing her while with someone. It's the first time I'm not alone. And I genuinely feel that. My eyes flick over to Nico, needing to see him just as badly as I want to see her.

And... that's when I fall apart. Because Nicolai Saint—a man I just met only weeks ago. A man who is *not* the biological father to my child, but loves her just the same, is crying. Openly and unabashedly. Tears are streaming down his grey and black stubbled cheeks.

I thought my heart would take years to mend. I thought the fractures in my soul, my very core, would never be fully repaired. But this man has proven my theory so completely wrong. He fluttered into my life on a strong wind and refused to be moved. He latched on to me, and my child, and vowed to care for us. And now, he's loving us. What I thought would take years, if not forever, has happened in less than a month.

Nico has made me believe again. In family. In happiness. In safety. *In love.*

I swallow down the thick lump in my throat and drag my eyes back to the monitor just as the doctor turns on the sound. The *woosh, woosh, woosh* of Pixie's heartbeat fills the room, only heightening the heavy emotions swirling around us.

"Holy shit," he breathes. Nico stands, leaning over me to get closer to the monitor. His eyes take in every feature, every detail. "Can I record this?"

Just when I thought I couldn't fall anymore.

"I'll make you a video," she says softly. "And print you some photos. Just enjoy this moment together." Nico glances down at me for the first time since Pixie made her presence known. "You know I love you now, right?"

I can't help it. I laugh, the sound echoed by Dr. Talbot's. Nico arches a brow to let me know he wasn't kidding. I choke down my laughter and nod. I'm not ready to say the words yet, but that doesn't mean I don't feel them. His eyes soften as though he knows.

"Do we want to know the gender?" she asks.

"No," we both say at the same time.

Nico grins, shaking his head. "We'll be surprised." He shrugs, turning his gaze back to Pixie just as she does a flip. "Maybe we'll find out early with the next one."

And that's how I find myself pressed up against a car door in the parking lot not even five minutes after leaving our appointment.

# Chapter Fourteen

## nicolai saint

I FEEL WILD. FRANTIC. My lips move from Tinsley's down to her jaw. Her neck. Her throat. Any and every inch of exposed skin gets touched by my lips, my tongue. I can't help it. I want to fucking devour her. Consume her. Seeing her in that room, her gorgeous belly on display. The marks that clearly show how much she's grown to accommodate our baby...and Pixie is *ours*. She's incredible. I've said it before, and I'll say it again. Tinsley Snow is a goddess.

And she's mine.

I groan, working my way down to her chest. Her shirt is white and fitted, showing off her heavy breasts and belly. She looks beautiful. So do her tits. Big. Full. *Mine.*

My mouth latches around one of her nipples, finding the soft cotton of her shirt already damp beneath my tongue. Her flavor, while muted, still explodes on my tastebuds. Sweet. So fucking sweet. Like sugary almond milk. I look up, locking eyes with her as I do something I've been aching to do for who knows how long. *I suck.* Tinsley's eyes widen. I expect her to freak out. To pull away. But that's not what my girl does. No. She shocks the hell out of me when she grips my hair and tugs me forward with a moan.

"Oh my god, Nico." She's panting. Shaking. Her thighs are restless. She's already close to cumming. I haven't gotten her off since that day in the hospital. I knew once I touched her again...had her in any way, I'd need her in every way. Like now.

I rip my mouth away, my cock so hard, I could bust through my zipper. "I need you, baby." She nods rapidly, gripping my head and dragging it up to hers. Our lips lock, and I groan when I realize she's tasting herself on my tongue—not just her cum, either. No, her milk, and fuck, if that doesn't do something crazy to my head. "Not here," I grunt, pulling away. "Not here, baby. At home."

Tinsley lets out a loud, stubborn whine and pulls at my belt. Holy shit, at this point, I may be fucking her in the car. I shake my head. No. Tinsley deserves better than that.

"Come on," I grunt, pulling her away from me and ushering her into my jeep. She whimpers the whole way home, and I continually have to bat her hands away. Not from my cock. Nope. From her pussy. I don't know how I manage to not careen into a ditch or pull over and fuck her on the side of the road. Apparently, I'm a Saint in more ways than one.

Tinsley reaches for her breasts, tweaking her nipples and moaning loudly. "No," I growl. "Mine." Jesus. I sound like a bear. I grip her hand, squeezing it tightly and resting it on the center console. "One more minute, Goddess. Then I swear to God, I'll fuck you so hard you forget how to breathe."

She sucks in a breath, turning her wide, needy eyes onto me. "I don't know what's wrong with me, Nico," she mutters, exhaling raggedly. "I've never been this turned on before."

"It's normal in late-stage pregnancy," I offer as I pull down the driveway. I can feel more than see her gaping at me. I shrug, picking up my speed as I plow through the fresh snow. See. *This* is why you need an off-roading vehicle. "I told you. I read all the books."

Everything after that is a blur. From the moment I pull into the garage until I have her cradled in my arms and up the stairs. All the way up to the point that my girl is on her back in our bed, panting and trembling with need.

Leaning down, I remove her shoes and socks, tossing them over my shoulder before slipping down her black maternity leggings and letting them join the growing pile. I shudder as my fingers grin the edges of her pink boyshorts. Tinsley lays limply, staring up at me with hooded eyes as though she can't possibly look away. Good. I want her to watch. Ever so fucking slowly, I slide them down her shapely thighs and over her feet. With her eyes locked on mine, I bring her panties up to my nose, unable to resist her delicious scent, and inhale deeply. My lids flutter closed as I release a low growl.

"Wow," she breathes. I smile, tossing the panties onto the nightstand for safekeeping. I have a feeling I'll be saving a lot of those in the future.

"Hold that thought." I grip her hand, pulling her to a seated position so I can remove her sweater. I meet her eyes as I find the edge of the soft material. I look for any hesitation. Any worry. My heart ricochets when I find none. Nothing but need, trust, and something else. Something much deeper. "I'm going to strip you down and devour you. Tell me it's okay. Tell me I can have you."

She pants, nodding slowly. "Please, Mr. Saint." *Holy shit.*

I practically rip her top from her body, knowing instantly that I'll need to buy her a new one. Fuck it. That's what money is for. I throw the tattered shirt on the floor before gently unclasping her bra.

Time slows as her simple white cotton bra falls to the bed, releasing her heavy breasts. My breath lodges in my chest, my lungs burning as I let my eyes drift from her face to the two milky globes I've fantasized about since that day in the diner.

"Shit," I choke out. Tinsley whimpers, shifting restlessly. I flick my gaze up to hers, finding her expression unreadable. *Compliment her, Nico, you idiot.* Christ. "You're stunning, Goddess. There are no words to describe how I feel about you right now." I press my lips to hers before gently pushing her onto her back and climbing to my feet. I look down at my girl, completely naked except for knee-highs, and take in her beauty. She's exquisite. Unbelievably exquisite.

She pants, her thighs rubbing together restlessly as her hands find her breasts. I click my tongue in disapproval, shaking my head. "Nico," she begs.

"No," I say softly. "Drop your knees and spread your thighs wide for me. Show me how wet you are for Daddy." She gasps, and I swallow a groan.

Fuck it. I'm already going to hell for tainting such a young, sweet innocent woman. Might as well add fuel to the hellfire with a little Daddy kink.

Tinsley does as I command, spreading her thighs wide and granting me the best view I've ever seen in my life. "Hands on the bed, baby. Let me see you." She hesitates but lets her hands fall to the comforter. She squeezes the grey blanket between her tiny fists, fighting her urge to hide.

"Good girl," I praise before letting my eyes drift and really take her in—inch by delicious inch.

Tinsley is a small woman. Her frame, her features. The largest part of her physically is her belly, and I find it mouthwatering. Her breasts are fuller than my hands can handle, but I'll enjoy every second of trying. Her areolas are a dusty rose color. Wide and round as they prepare to feed our child. Her nipples, however—those are hard and puckered as they prepare to feed *me*.

Her skin is covered in red and purple stretchmarks from her hips to her chest. Her breasts have pink lines coating the underside of them. Against her pale skin, the marks stand out, drawing my attention. They're beautiful. My heart swells with pride at the sight of them. My eyes continue their downward journey, finally landing at the sweet place between her thighs. Her cunt is covered in light curls that are nearly invisible. Not that I care either way.

Dress it up or down. Decorate it however the fuck you want. Toss some tinsel and Christmas lights down there for fun. Doesn't matter. No man worth a damn will be thinking about anything but licking it from front to back, side to side, before stuffing it full of his fingers, cock, and in my case, cum. Pussy's are priceless, but Tinsley's is Heaven. And it's all fucking mine.

"Fuck, Goddess," I practically snarl, ripping my shirt over my head. I lose my clothes with zero finesse, stumbling twice when I try to remove my jeans before my shoes. Tinsley doesn't laugh, though. She does nothing but lay there, spread wide for me, her eyes locked on my body with as much awe and adoration as I feel for her.

When I finally lower my boxer briefs, her mouth drops open. I may not be a huge man, but I am a big man. "Holy shit," she murmurs, licking her lips before flicking her eyes up to mine. "That won't fit."

I growl, fisting my cock. I'm throbbing harder than I've ever been in my entire life. Partly because I've refused to jack off since the diner, but mostly because of her. My woman. My Tinsley.

"It'll fucking fit, baby. I promise you that." I kick my boxers from my ankles and give my cock one last squeeze, willing it to calm the fuck down before I bust all over her feet. "If it means I have to work your pretty pussy up with my tongue and fingers, stretching you until you practically take my entire fist, then so be it. I'm in no rush."

The second I'm fully naked, I'm on her. My mouth and tongue touch every inch of her body, starting with her feet and working my way up, up, up. I move slowly, enjoying this first, knowing things will change after this. For the better, no doubt. But still. It's my first time getting to have the greatest gift on earth, and I'll be fucked if I don't worship her the way she deserves.

"I need you, Nico," she pants. "Please, please, please."

I softly bite her thigh, relishing in the needy whine she releases. "Not yet."

I continue on my upward path, purposefully skipping over her pussy, even though doing so feels like it might kill me. When I reach her belly, we both stop breathing. My eyes meet hers as I straddle her thighs with mine. My cock is solid and weeping between us, but we both ignore it. My tongue darts out, licking a trail up one of her larger stretchmarks. Tinsley freezes, her eyes wide. I lick a path up the entire line before pressing a kiss to it. I repeat the process until I've thoroughly shown her my gratitude for this gift. Not just Pixie, but trusting me enough to let me in.

By the time I'm done, she's shaking and crying silent tears. I climb up her body, keeping my weight off of hers.

"Your body is a temple, Goddess. I am in awe of you." She squeezes her eyes shut, and I palm her cheek, brushing it softly. "I'm obsessed with you, Tinsley Snow. Every inch of you, inside and out." I tap my finger on her temple. "Your beautiful mind." I slide my hand down, pressing it against her chest. "Your huge heart. A heart I have no doubt tripled in size the second you found out you were pregnant." I press my lips to hers once more, muttering against them. "And if it's not evident by the solid cock practically stabbing your belly right now, I'm obsessed with your body. You're growing our child, baby. You're fucking incredible."

"Ours," she chokes out.

I nod against her cheek. "That child may not be biologically half mine, but she is ours. If you want that. I know I'll love her just as much, if not more than I love you because you created her. In heart, mind, and spirit, that baby is your twin. And because of that, I know she'll be just as perfect as her mama." I kiss her then, pouring my love and desire into her. Showing her with my lips and tongue how badly I want her. She groans, biting down on my lower lip. I grunt, pulling away. "Now let me show you what it's like to be worshiped like the goddess you fucking are."

And then, I give into the desire to taste her. I'm momentarily torn between what I want in my mouth first, but one glance at the needy look on my girl's face and I know my wants will have to wait. Not that sucking her clit and fucking her pretty pussy with my tongue is a hardship.

I slip between her thighs and waste no more time before diving in. My tongue lashes out, stroking her from asshole to clit. Her hips shoot off the bed as I moan around her flavor. Sweet. So fucking sweet. Wrapping my arms around her thighs, I tug her back down, keeping her exactly where I want her, and *feast*.

"Nico," she cries out as I latch around her hard clit. I find I love the sound of her screaming, so I repeat the movement, sucking even harder. "More," Tinsley begs. "Please. I feel so empty." Thank fucking God I already read about pregnancy and sex, so I know what's safe. Otherwise, I'd been freaking the hell out.

"I've got you, baby," I coo, flattening my tongue and drinking down her wetness. She's drenched, and I'll be damned if I waste a drop. I slide a finger into her dripping hole, groaning when I slip right in. I quickly add a second finger, finding a slight amount of resistance. I curl my fingers upward, massaging that hidden spot I know will set her off. She instantly shoots off the bed, screaming and flooding my hand with her release. *So damn wet.* "Such a good fucking girl, Goddess. Drenching Daddy's hand so he can stretch your pretty cunt out."

"Fuck," she moans, writhing against me.

I chuckle against her skin. "That's the plan."

I've gotten no less than five orgasms from her by the time I've worked my way up to four fingers spreading her wide for me. I want her soft and comfortable while she takes my cock. For a moment, I get distracted thinking about how she'd look with my entire fist inside her pussy. Stretching her to her limits, preparing her for our baby. I swallow down a harsh groan and shake my head. Kissing her clit one last time, I slip my fingers from her pussy and crawl back up her body.

Tinsley's sweaty and sated, but she has an adorable sleepy smile spread across her face that I immediately love. "You good, baby?"

She nods slowly. "So good."

Grinning, I bring my dripping fingers to her lips. "Then suck."

And that's the exact moment I realize Tinsley Snow doesn't do well with having shit shoved down her throat. "Aww, fuck," I grunt, stroking her back in soothing circles until she stops gagging. Well. I guess blowjobs are off the table.

Her eyes water as she blinks up at me. "I'm so sorry."

I cock a brow at her. "For?"

She scoffs, settling back on the bed. "Ruining the moment."

I bark a laugh and lean back on my thighs, stroking my leaking cock. "Does this look like you've ruined a damn thing? My dick is liable to fall off if I'm not in you soon."

She whimpers, biting the inside of her cheek. "I'll practice,"

I growl. "The only cock sucking practice you'll do is on me, but listen to me when I tell you that it's not necessary. As long as I can suck and fuck your pussy and maybe someday your tits, I'm a happy man, Goddess. You got me?"

She sucks in a breath. "You want to fuck my boobs?"

I groan, and a splash of precum drizzles from my dick just from hearing those words leave her lips. "I have visions of fucking your milky tits while my dick's covered in your breastmilk." I shrug when she gapes at me. "I find that when it comes to you, there are no boundaries to my fantasies. You may not be ready to hear it yet, but I'm turned on by every inch of you, and the thought of drinking down your sweet cream has me ready to blow." I shake my head. "There's just something about seeing you pregnant and carrying a life, Tinsley. It's fucking incredible. And knowing that your beautiful breasts will feed our children—give them the nourishment they need to be healthy—*fuck baby*. It's sexy as hell."

Her mouth opens and closes before she groans and looks down. I follow her gaze, finding tiny trickles of white liquid leaking from her nipples. I release a moan I didn't know I was capable of. I swallow, my mouth watering. "Is that okay, Tinsley? Can I suck you?"

She licks her lips and nods slowly. "It's not regular breastmilk. It's colostrum right now. It's probably not that sweet."

Crawling over her body, I decide I'll be the judge of that. Leaning down, I exhale a raged breath before lapping up the spilled liquid. I don't know if it's how turned on I am or just because I've been craving this so badly, but the flavor immediately explodes on my tongue. Sweet and salty. I groan, my eyes fluttering closed as I dip down for another taste.

"What's it like?" she whispers, her body twitching beneath mine. "Is it okay?" I look up at her, answering without words as I wrap my lips around her taught nipple and *suck...hard*. Tinsley moans, her hands immediately shooting out to cradle my head. "Oh, fuck, Nico. That feels so good, baby."

I shudder, sucking her harder. There's not a lot of milk, but it's enough for me to know that this is definitely something I want more of. I pop off her breast when the liquid stops flowing freely and switch to the other, repeating the process. This is what Heaven tastes like. Tinsley's gingerbread-flavored skin, her sweet and salty cream tinged with the remnants of her pussy juice on my tongue. Fucking Heaven. If I died right now, I'd know exactly what's waiting for me on the other side.

Her hips are restlessly writing beneath my spread thighs, making her bump collide with my cock repeatedly. Tinsley is moaning as though I'm fucking her, and I'm pretty sure she's seconds from cumming without even being touched.

*Fuck that.*

With one final suck, I swallow down the warm liquid, savoring every drop. I release her breast and look down, finding both nipples pink and purple from how hard I was latched on. I should apologize, but I won't. The sight of her covered in my marks awakens something primal inside of me. It's about to get way worse. I drop my mouth to hers, kissing the ever-loving shit out of my girl. I thrust my tongue between her lips, forcing her to taste the heady cocktail that is Tinsley Snow. I pull away, my forehead resting against hers.

"I'm clean, and I haven't had sex in a very fucking long time. I'm not using condoms." I shiver at the thought of feeling her wrapped around me. "I want nothing between us. Ever."

She swallows. "I'm clean, too." She looks away, but I interrupt her before she can speak. She doesn't need to go there. Never again.

"I know, baby. I know."

Dropping to her side, I maneuver us, so I'm spooning behind her, recalling one of the preferred late-stage pregnancy positions I'd found in the baby books I read. Wrapping one arm beneath her neck, I bring her in close, cradling her against me like the precious gift she is. I gently tap her ass cheek.

"Lift up for me, Goddess. I need to be inside you." She arches her back and lifts her outer thigh. Gripping my leaking cock, I slide between her drenched pussy lips until I hit her clit. We both groan at the feeling, and I nearly bust all over her. Only the desire to fill her sweet cunt with my cum, making her from the inside out, stops me.

"You ready?" I murmur. Tinsley tilts her head back, finding my lips. "I love you, Tinsley Snow," I whisper.

I swallow her gasp with my mouth and use her shock to slide inside of her in one brutal thrust. She cries out, and I give her a moment to adjust. Fuck, who am I kidding? We both need it. She pulses around me, making me growl into our kiss. When she finally shoves her hips back, I know she's ready. Lifting her thigh, I brace her leg in the crook of my arm, opening her up to me. And then, I fuck her. Long, hard and slow strokes, again and again, until she's screaming and begging.

"More, Nico. Please. Harder. Please." Tinsley whines and shakes, but I ignore her, refusing to let this be over so quickly. "Please."

"No, Goddess," I grunt, lifting her leg higher until it's practically by her ears. "Not yet. Not until you cum for me again."

She shakes her head, panting. "I can't."

"Yes, you fucking can. Rub your clit for me. Rub it hard while I own your pussy. While I claim it." She groans, tipping her head back onto my chest, but she does as I say. "Do you like that? Knowing this pussy belongs to me now? Knowing that no other man will ever touch what's mine again?"

She whimpers but doesn't answer. I pause in my incessant thrusting, waiting her out. She swallows. "Yes."

I pump in once more, then pause again. "Who do you belong to, Tinsley?" I thrust in again, harder, faster. "Who?"

"You, Nico," she cries.

*Oh, fuck yes.*
I pound into her pussy like my life depends on it, chasing both of our releases. I reach around with the hand under her neck and palm her heavy tit. I squeeze gently, knowing how sensitive she is, before pinching her taut nipple between my fingers. She cries out, and I groan as I feel her cream trickle down my palm. Fucking hell.

"That's right. You belong to me now, and no one, *no one*, will ever fucking hurt you again. Do you hear me? I would die before I let someone else put their hands on you." I press my lips to her neck, accentuating my next words with a deep grind against her ass as I roll my fingers around her wet nipple. "You're safe now. You can let go, baby."

Tinsley screams as she cums, squeezing my cock so hard she forces my orgasm from my balls before I'm even ready. I shout into her neck, trembling as though I've been electrocuted. Holy shit. That's never happened to me before.

"Fuck, fuck, fuck," she whimpers, her fingers still dancing along her clit as she rides out a very long, very wet orgasm.

"Such a good fucking girl, Goddess," I breathe. "You took Daddy's cum so good, didn't you?" I murmur the words feeling drunk and delirious.

Tinsley lets out a puff of air and giggles as her body finally relaxes. My cock pulses repeatedly inside of her. I can feel both of our releases leaking out down her ass and my balls, but I don't care. I'm not moving. Having Tinsley in my arms, my dick inside of her is the best feeling in the world. Nearly. I gently lower her thigh, massaging her muscle and hip before settling my palm on her belly. I press my lips to the back of her head and just breathe her in.

"Are you okay? Was I too rough?" She exhales a long, happy sigh and nestles deeper into me, bracing her tiny hands under her head.

"No. It was perfect." She sounds exhausted. "Thank you."

I chuckle, rubbing her belly. "Don't you dare thank me for the single best experience of my life—so far."

She shakes with silent laughter. "Oh yeah? Got something else on your calendar that you think will outdo this, Mr. Saint?"

I bite her neck and growl. She screeches. I lick the small hurt, then decide I want to cover her in hickeys. Not right now, though. Doing something else I learned in the baby books, I scoop under her heavy belly and lift slightly, taking some pressure from her back.

"Yes," I breathe. "As a matter of fact, I do."

"Oh yeah?" she murmurs, groaning in appreciation.

"Yep. Her birth will no doubt be the best day of my life. I already know it." I pause, thinking that through. "But, it might have to battle it out with our wedding day."

She giggles, shaking her head. "So confident, aren't we."

I scoff. "Abso-fucking-lutely." I know I can't make my feelings for Tinsley any clearer. This has all been a whirlwind at lightning speed. I don't blame her for being weary. All I can do now is wait her out and make sure she has no reason to doubt me.

We fall into silence, and at one point, I think she's fallen asleep, but she shifts, pressing her ass into my groin. I groan, my half-mast cock pulsing inside of her with interest. "Uh, Nico?" she murmurs. I mutter a random sound. She snickers. "Don't you want to—I don't know. Evacuate my vagina?"

I growl, tugging her closer. "Nope. I'm perfectly fine right here."

"What happens when I need to pee?"

"Do you need to pee, Tinsley?" I murmur, my lips brushing against her hair.

She sighs. "Not yet, but it's only a matter of time."

"Then wake me up when that happens. Go pee. And then I'll fuck you again, and we'll go right back to sleep with my dick swaddled in your perfect pussy." I kiss her head. "Get used to it, baby. My dick has been cold for 46 years, and it just discovered the perfect place to keep it warm."

"Jesus," she mutters. "Already starting with the dad jokes, I see."

I grin against her. At least she's finally catching on.

---

I wake up and immediately notice the cold spot in front of me where my girl used to be. My eyes snap open as I frantically look for her.

"Tins?" I murmur, my voice thick with sleep. The room is dark except for the moonlight pooling in from the floor-to-ceiling windows. There are blackout curtains, but I've noticed my girl likes to look at the backyard. I crawl from bed, buck ass naked, ready to hunt her ass down. I barely make it a step when I hear it. The quiet sniffle. Then another. My heart rate picks up as panic fills me. "Tinsley?"

I quickly check the bathroom and closet before my eyes land on the third door. The one, to my knowledge, she hasn't discovered yet. Apparently, that's changed. Smiling, I open the nursery door, immediately finding Tinsley bundled up in the grey and white rocking chair, wearing nothing but my t-shirt and a tear-stained face.

I momentarily get distracted by the sight. Her, in my clothes, in our baby's room. A wave of possession washes over me, and the need to growl the word *mine* lodges in my throat. I swallow it down and lean against the doorframe, crossing my arms over my chest. My dick is steadily hardening, and I feel it slap against my thigh as I cross my ankles.

"Goddess?" I murmur softly. She blinks rapidly but doesn't startle. Her arms are banded around the pink dragon stuffed animal I placed in Pixie's crib.

She swallows loudly. "When?"

She doesn't need to explain her question. I knew it was coming. I was just hoping for a better reaction than this. My eyes glide around the light pink nursery adorned with white trim, soft cream rugs, and white furniture. The decorators brought my vision to life. Quickly, I might add. This nursery may have been a placeholder, but there is no doubt now who it's intended for. The magical fantasy room is meant for a real-life pixie. If there was still any question about that, I put her nickname above her crib in sparking pink letters.

Looking back at my girl, I smile and shrug. "The first day I saw you, I made the call."

She tilts her head to the side. "At the staff meeting?"

"No, baby," I murmur. "A few days before that, I walked in on you asleep in Candy's office."

"What?" she chokes out. "That was the first day I ever stepped foot in Wonderland, though."

Sighing, I push off the doorframe and kneel before her. Tucking her wild, stringy hair behind her ear, I say a silent thank you to whoever is listening that she doesn't pull away. "The heart wants what it wants."

She stares at me for a long moment before falling into a fit of giggles. "Did you just quote Selena Gomez?"

I scoff. "She's a boss, baby. Don't talk smack."

"Oh lord," she groans, tipping her head back. "Don't try to be cool, grandpa."

I smack her bare thigh hard enough to make her yelp. "That's Mr. Grandpa to you." Tinsley chuckles before falling silent again. "Are you freaked out?"

She exhales a shaky breath, her eyes darting around the room. "No," she whispers. "I know I should be, but I'm not." She looks down at me once more and smiles. "I'm speechless."

Tinsley passes me the stuffed animal and I toss it back in the crib to my left before turning back to her. Her hands are cradling her belly and she has an odd expression on her face that I can't quite make out.

"What is it?" I murmur, rubbing my fingers up and down her thighs.

She says nothing as she reaches down and grabs my hand, bringing it join hers on her belly. My brow furrows in confusion but then, I feel it. My eyes widen and my jaw drops open. "Is that what I think it is?" Tinsley gives me a soft look and nods. "Holy shit." As if in response to my voice, Pixie moves again. It's not strong like a kick or punch. More of a swish and bump. Like she's rolling around in her mama.

"She was asleep, but now she's pretty active," Tinsley whispers. "She likes it in this room."

I swallow, letting my eyes drift shut as I absorb feeling my girl move for the first time. Inching my knees forward, I drop my head on her knees and cup her belly with both hands, eager for more. Tinsley lets a heavy breath whoosh out as she begins to run her fingers through my hair as we enjoy Pixie's midnight antics. We stay like that, in comfortable bliss until I've lost track of time and my thighs have fallen asleep.

Tinsley tugs my hair slightly and murmurs, "She's asleep."

I groan, shifting on my legs kiss her belly. "Goodnight, babygirl."

"Thank you," Tinsley chokes out, her voice full of emotion. "Thank you for everything. I can't even describe how grateful I am for you, Nicolai Saint."

Ignoring her thanks, I press my lips to her nose, cheeks, and eyes. I pepper her face in kisses until I pull another beautiful laugh out of her. "I did good?"

"So good," she pants. "Let me show you how happy I am—" she breaks off, pulling away. Pressing me back by my shoulders, she stands. Slowly, so fucking slowly, she slides my shirt from her head, leaving her completely bare, her delicious pussy right in front of my face. "*Daddy.*"

Well, shit.

# Chapter Fifteen

## TINSLEY SNOW

THE FOLLOWING WEEK, I'M finally feeling the late stages of pregnancy enough that I decide to stop working after today. With the accommodations I'd agreed upon with Candy and Nico, my job duties are incredibly minimal. All I've been doing is sitting at the register, ringing customers up with the help of another staff member. Most of the time, it's one of the younger volunteers. If I'm not doing that, I'm in the office, working on the books or administrative tasks for

Candy. A job she likely chose just because her office has a bathroom and a couch. Good call, too, because at this point, if I'm not napping, I'm peeing. Or eating. Or begging Nico for sex.

Which he gives me...often.

Something shifted in both of us after that first time. We're insatiable. Every single time, he insists on worshipping me. Ensuring I've cum again and again before he makes love to me. It's sweet. Really, it is. But I want to be ravished.

No. I want to be *fucked*.

That's why I skipped out of work early today to go on a secret mission in the mall that Wonderland is attached to. It was easy, and Candy was all for giving an early final day. I'm making enough money now to splurge, especially since Nico refuses to let me contribute to household costs.

The stubborn asshole.

I smile to myself. Nico is anything but an asshole. He's perfect.

"What's got you lookin' like that, Darlin'?" Lottie quips, hip-bumping me. Except her hip reaches my ribs, and I stumble to the side. "Oops. Sorry," she chuckles, sounding anything but sorry.

I sigh, straightening my elf costume that's busting at the seams these days. "Oh, nothing," I murmur, my lips twitching as butterflies consume me. That's all it takes. Just one thought of him. My Nico. And I'm a loved-up puddle of Christmas pudding.

She scoffs, swinging her bags at her sides. "Liar," she mutters. "I'm sure it has everything to do with a certain sexy Santa and his package if you know what I mean."

I grumble, rolling my eyes. "The entire mall knew what you meant, Lott." But still, I smirk. "And yes. His very *big* package."

"Ooooph," she groans, shaking her head. "One. That's not something I needed to know. And two. Good for you, Sugar. You needed a good dickin' down."

"Christ," I hiss, my eyes darting around to the people near us. It's almost Christmas, and the mall is packed with families. I shoot her a withering glare. "Keep it down, will ya? Or at least PG."

Lottie grimaces but clucks her tongue in disapproval. "I wouldn't have agreed to a girl's afternoon if I knew sex talk would be off the table."

My eyes shoot heavenward as I pray for patience. "It's not off the table, Lottie. Just—" I break off with a groan as Pixie begins to bounce on my bladder.

Lottie gives me a sympathetic, knowing look. "How's our girl doing?"

I nod, rubbing the small ache. "She's great. Our doctor's appointment was," I pause, blushing as I recall just how amazing it was. And what came afterward. *Me. Again and again.* "Wonderful," I finally say, shaking away the lusty thoughts. Something that's nearly impossible these days. "The doctor said she's doing perfectly. My adjusted due date is now the 20th, though."

"That's what, five days early?" she asks. I bob my head and shift my heavy backpack. "Well, that's normal. Especially around this time."

"Yep," I agree, popping the *p*. "That's what the doctor said. Pixie's out of space, and she could come anytime in the next few weeks and be okay."

Lottie sucks in a gasp and squeezes my shoulder to halt me mid-step. She bends down to whisper, "Are you ready for that?" My brows furrowed in question. She scoffs. "To shoot a baby out of your cooter, Tinsley. You do know you have to do that, right?"

I groan, shoving her away. "Of course I do. I'm not an idiot." I give her a sidelong look. "No one says cooter, Lot." I shudder. "Gross."

"I hope you been doin' your Kegels. Stretching yourself." Now I'm the one to freeze as I gape at her. She tuts. "That's what all the best midwives say you should be doin' around this time. Gentle, slow vaginal stretching to help with the birth. Especially since it's your first baby."

"For what?" I choke out, my heartbeat racing and my stomach turning. I might lose the delicious mall pretzel I just inhaled.

She turns, picking up her pace once more as though she knows I'm seconds from needing a toilet. "So you don't tear, Darlin'. Obviously."

I'm still processing her words when we reach the Wonderland mall entrance. Lottie turns to me. She shifts her assortments of bags on her forearms and squeezes my shoulders. "Really, though. You're good, right? Happy with Nicolai? It's not too fast?"

I smile, my eyes burning. I'm so freaking thankful I stumbled across this amazing town. "So damn happy, Lott." I shrug helplessly, unable to find the words to explain how perfect everything is.

Her shoulders drop as she sighs heavily, her cheeks puffing up from her massive grin. "I'm so happy for you, Darlin'. I'm glad you found him and that Jackson found you." I arch a brow. She cackles and winks at me before stepping away. "I told you, Tinsley. This place is alive with the

Christmas spirit. It knows when we need a miracle." She turns but not before shouting, "Don't forget what I said about the cooter-shooter."

"Elf off," I shout back before muttering, "Well, jingle balls." Apparently, I need to do some research.

---

I've just barely made it back to work, my packages discretely tucked into my leather backpack purse, when I see him. Nico is pounding down the escalator, not even waiting for the conveyer belt to reach the ground. His eyes are wide and frantic, immediately filling me with dread.

I freeze in place as his wild eyes lock onto mine. "What is it? What's wrong? Has something happened?"

Nico collides with me, his hands gripping my cheeks roughly. He smashes his lips to mine and releases a shuddering breath. I sink into him, my knees weak at the feeling of his body against mine. A feeling I love way too much. He rips his mouth from mine and presses our foreheads together.

"Where were you?" his voice is choked up. My eyes narrow in confusion. That's why he's freaking out. I open my mouth, but he shakes his head. He looks angrier than I've ever seen him before, but I'm not scared. Intrinsically, I know he would never hurt me. "Goddammit, Tinsley. You can't do that to me. I showed up early to surprise you, and you were gone." His eyes find my belly at the same time as his hands. He palms me softly. "Is she okay?"

Sheesh. He's going to kill me. I know it. I'm going to die from his sweet affection.

I smile softly, covering his hands when I feel her rouse from her nap. "I'm perfect, baby. I just went out to buy your Christmas present with Lottie. I'm sorry I didn't call, but—" I shrug. "I wanted to surprise you also."

He opens his mouth, his features softening, but then Pixie makes herself known. Just like last time, Nico gasps. His face fills with a reverence I never thought I'd see as he takes in the moment. She kicks harshly, and I wince but don't move, letting him enjoy this. Moments like this will be engrained in my memory forever. I just know it.

She settles down once more, and he waits a solid five minutes before finally releasing me. We probably look like idiots standing in the middle of Wonderland, but I don't care. I've found that when it comes to this...to what we're building here...nothing else matters. His eyes flick up to mine, and that previous anger, the panic, is replaced with heat. Burning hot need.

"Don't ever do that to me again, Goddess. You got it?" I nod, the command in his words leaving me breathless. "Good. Let's go."

Before I can respond, he's dragging me back to the escalator. Though he's pulling me along quickly, he's careful not to hurt me, always keeping me safe first and foremost. Nico practically sprints to the office, the door slamming against the wall as he throws it open. He gently pushes me through before flicking the lock. The sound is like a gunshot in the silent room.

Nico crosses the space in record time, ripping his shirt off as goes. He kicks off his shoes and backs me up until my ass hits Candy's desk. His hands slide up my exposed thighs, clearly not in the mood to fuck around.

"I need you, Tinsley. Need you so fucking badly, I'm practically starving for you." His hand cups my pussy roughly, and I gasp, arching onto my tippy toes.

"Starving for this juicy pussy." His other hand finds my right breast, tweaking it softly before pinching my nipple with unnerving accuracy.

"Starving for your sweet cream." We both groan when my milk releases in a gentle trickle, nothing but his words and touch to set me off. His palm grinds against my clit, and my hips thrust forward, needing more pressure. Nico bends down and sucks my dripping nipple into his mouth, sucking harshly as though he truly is starving. Or parched, apparently. "So damn good, baby." His tongue runs over my velvet dress, lapping up my flavor.

"Nico," I whimper, gripping his hair as I begin to fuck his palm. I'm already so close. *This.* This is what he does to me.

"I crave you, Tinsley Snow. I crave you every second of every day. Your body." He accentuates the word by flicking my clit. I moan loudly. "Your flavor." He sucks me between his lips again, granting himself another hit of my breastmilk. "Your fucking soul."

Then he's kissing me again. His mouth is sweet, lightly tinted with the sweet creamy taste of milk. Nico slides my panties down to my thighs before ripping his mouth from mine. He spins me around, forcing me to brace myself on the desk with my elbows. He's careful to keep space between the harsh wood and my belly but I still find myself swelling with panic. Not at this. Him or what we're doing but...I suck in a breath, my body freezing in place. Nico notices immediately.

"Goddess?" he murmurs, but I can barely hear him against the whooshing in my ears as flashbacks from another time, another man, flit through my brain. "Tinsley, baby. Please."

The terrified begging sound in his voice snaps me out of it. It's then that I realize I'm in his arms, and we're sitting on the couch. His palm rests against my cheek, gently wiping away the tears streaming down my face. I suck in a sharp breath and shiver.

"I'm okay." Nico's jaw pulses, and his eyes narrow.

"Try that a-fucking-gain, please. This time, without the lie." I squeeze my eyes shut and work to control my breathing.

*Shit.* I can't believe I just had a panic attack. That hasn't happened in...well...months. "The desk," I whisper, unable to say anything else. Nico tenses beneath me, his hard cock quickly wilting, taking my arousal with it.

"The desk," he states. I nod. He shudders, letting out something akin to a growl. I drop my head to his shoulder, surprisingly finding comfort with his body against mine when previously, a panic attack caused the exact opposite. "I'm so fucking sorry, baby."

I nod against him, his beard brushing my forehead in a way I find relaxing. "I know. But it's not your fault." I swallow thickly. "I haven't had sex since then and that time," I break off, feeling slightly embarrassed but mostly just sad. Sad about the entire situation.

Nico sucks in a sharp breath. His hand grips my jaw as he softly turns me to face him. "Baby," he mutters, sounding sick. "Was the assault your first time?" The tears pick up as I nod. "*Fuck, Tinsley.*"

He bundles me in his arms, his body rocking soothingly as if he's trying to comfort the both of us. The whole time, he says sweet words of adoration and praise that have me breaking. Breaking for the first time since it happened. Don't get me wrong... I've cried. I've cried a lot over the last nine months. But every time, I've forced myself to stop. To get it together. To be strong for Pixie. Now...now I don't have to be. I can fall, knowing Nico will catch me.

We stay like that for a long time. Well beyond when my tears have dried up, and his gentle sways have stopped. Peeling my eyes open, I lean back to find his gaze. Nico's already staring down at me, his eyes so full of love, it sucks the breath right from my lungs.

"I love you, Nicolai Saint." It's the first time I've said the words back to him. The first time I felt brave enough to give in to this fully. I trust him with my life. More than that, I trust him with Pixies. I know this is it. It's him and me and her and any other children we create together. A family.

Nico looks pained for a second, the force of my words hitting him like a sucker punch. Then, he's smiling. His grin is so huge his cheeks dimple and turn pink. His lips find mine. It's soft. Slow. An affirmation. A thank you. A reciprocation. "I know," he murmurs, his beard ghosting over my jaw. "I'm glad you've finally caught up."

I shift on his lap, my legs falling to either side of his thighs. My skirt pulls around my waist as I settle over his cock. Using my grip on his shoulders to hold myself steady, I grind down on his rapidly returning erection.

"Do you love me, Mr. Saint?" I whisper, looking up at him from beneath my lashes. I bite down on my lower lip in a way that I know undoes him.

Nico groans. His hands squeeze my hips below my belly as he thrusts up into my aching pussy.

"You know I do," he growls.

I swallow, releasing my lip with a pop. "Say it," I whisper.

His eyelids flutter at the pure sex in my voice. "I love you, Goddess. So damn much."

I rock harder, practically fucking his jean-covered dick. "Then prove it."

Nico snaps...*finally*.

# Chapter Sixteen

## TINSLEY SNOW

With one hand, Nico cuffs the back of my neck and tugs me forward, crashing our mouths together. His other slips beneath my skirt and wraps around my thin, worn cotton panties. His tongue presses against the seam of my lips, demanding access. Access I greedily give him, practically sucking him into my mouth. Nico growls and pulls on my underwear until the telltale sound of the material ripping spills through the room. Cold air hits my swollen, wet pussy, making me shiver.

"Wow, that was hot," I pant, my chest rising and falling rapidly. He groans in agreement, his teeth sliding down the exposed flesh of my throat. Nico bites and sucks as though he's trying to prove a point. He yanks at the collar of my dress and huffs indistinguishable words of frustration. Chuckling, I gently bat him away and lean back on his knees. "Let me," I breathe.

Reaching down, I grip the base of my new dress and slowly lift it over my head. The velvet elf costume slips from my fingers and drifts to the floor, leaving me in my socks and booties.

Nico groans, dropping his head back on the couch. His palms slide up my thighs to rest on my hips as he openly devours me.

"Are you trying to kill me, Goddess? Why the fuck aren't you wearing a bra?" he grunts. I drop down on his dick, and the thick material of his pants creates delicious friction against my clit, making me whimper.

I roll my hips, palming my heavy breasts. "They ache," I sigh. "Nico, I need you to fuck me, baby. Please. I need it hard."

He leans forward, shoving my hands away with a growl. He grips my chin, forcing me to meet his hard stare. "Do you need it hard, Goddess? Or do you just need to feel full?"

Shuddering, I shrug. I don't know what I need. I'm new at this. I just know I feel so completely empty without him, and ever since our first time, I've become insatiable. I want him all the time. I want him owning me, claiming, filling me. It's reckless and idiotic, but I don't care. I'm his, and he's mine, and nothing compares to the feeling of us together.

"I don't know," I murmur, then groan when he wraps his thick lips around my nipple. I immediately cup his head, bringing him in tightly against my skin. The feeling of his short stubble combined with his hot tongue as he sucks from my breast has me grinding down harder on his solid cock below me. But it's not enough. Frustrated, I cry out. "I'm empty, Nico."

He pops off, licking his lips and swallowing a small gulp of liquid. His eyes flutter in ecstasy. "I know you are," he coos, switching to my other breast. "But not for long."

One hand anchors me upright with a firm grip on my hip, and the other slips between my drenched lips. The first brush of his fingers across my clit has me gasping. But when Nico slides one finger and then two into my drenched core, I go off like a rocket. My ass shoots up in the air. Only his grip keeps me in place. "There she is. There's my good fucking girl. Look at you, cumming for Daddy."

"Fuck, Nico," I cry. His fingers pump inside of me slowly, prolonging my release, but I quickly realize it's still not enough. I grip his shoulders for leverage and lift myself up before dropping back down. His palm hits my clit with every thrust, sending sparks down my spine. "More," I beg.

"Shit, Goddess." He picks me up an inch, enough to give him room to pull out. I whine, and Nico chuckles darkly at the sound. "Shh," he murmurs. "Be patient while I stretch your pretty pussy."

Lottie's words ricochet through my brain, making me pause. My fingernails dig into his shoulders, drawing a groan from his lips. His eyes lift to mine just as three fingers slip back in. The burn is there, but it's not bad. If anything, the warmth turns me on more.

I swallow, wondering if I should tell Nico about my conversation with Lottie. Would he think it's weird? I mean...he *is* talking about stretching me. How stretched did she mean? How often? And am I supposed to find it so damn hot?

"What is it, Tinsley?" he asks, his entire body going still. "Did I do something?"

Dammit. He thinks he's triggered me again. I shake my head, running my fingers through his hair lovingly. "No," I breathe. Rolling my shoulders back, I decide to come out with it. "Lottie mentioned it was good to start," I swallow a groan. "Stretching myself. You know. To make my delivery easier."

Nico doesn't move. Doesn't speak. He barely breathes as he stares at me. His eyes flick down to between my spread thighs, where his fingers are still just barely breaching my entrance. His body vibrates. "And what do you think about that?" he mumbles, licking his lips before meeting my eyes. His are burning and nearly black. "Do you want me to stretch your tiny pussy, Goddess? Fuck you with my tongue and fist until your dripping down my forearm?"

Unable to respond, I reach between us and grip his wrist, prepared to shove him back inside me. Nico growls, tugging my hand away and bracing it behind my back, causing my chest to thrust forward. "If you can't keep your hands to yourself, I'll have to tie you up," he tuts, shaking his head. My eyes widen, and I bite down on my lip. Nico chuckles. "You'd like that, wouldn't you?

Goddamn, you're perfect." He licks a path up between my tits and bites down on my jaw. "My perfect dirty girl."

With that, he thrusts his hand upward, impaling me on his thick fingers. I cry out, my back arching in pleasure. Nico grunts, releasing my arm and guiding it back to his shoulder. "Use me, Tinsley," he commands. "Fuck yourself on my hand. Take as much as you want for as long as you need. You're in control. You on top. Me beneath you, worshipping you the way you deserve." I swallow at his words, understanding what he's giving me right now. "Take it. Take every piece of me. It's yours."

"Nico," I breathe. My core throbs in time with my heartbeat, clenching and unclenching around him. I take in the soft, loving expression on his face. The heat and desire in his eyes. And the rock-hard cock between my thighs. And then, I let go.

I ride Nico's hand as though it's his cock. I fuck myself on him with abandon. My head tossed back, my heavy breasts bouncing with every fall and rise of my body. My wide belly is between us, and it brushes against his bare stomach in time with my movements. I embrace it all. And for the first time, I truly feel like the Goddess he claims me to be.

Nico latches onto my breast, curves his fingers, finds my g-spot with unnerving accuracy, and presses his thumb to my clit. That's all it takes to send me into yet another orgasm. This one isn't as long or intense as the first. It's burning. Deep. I can feel something building inside of me. Something…more.

He releases me, licking me clean. "What do you need, baby?" he breathes, his voice raspy and pained. "Tell me, and it's yours."

"More," I pant, lifting my shaky legs. Nico obliges immediately, removing his slick fingers from my core before working them back in, adding another.

Nico groans. "Look at you, Tinsley. Fucking hell. Do you feel that?" He shifts his hand, swirling it around, *back and forth, back and forth*. Stretching, tugging. It's the most delicious burn I've ever felt in my life. It's not painful. It's searing. Intimate. I feel connected to him in new and indescribable ways. "You're doing it, baby. Holy shit."

I look down and whimper when my bump keeps me from seeing what he's seeing. Noticing my frustration, he shifts us on the couch, his hand never leaving my core until we're horizontal. Nico bends his knees, giving me a place to lean back. His head rests on Candy's pile of pillows, keeping him close to my body.

"Hang on," he grunts, tugging his phone from his pocket. I suck in a gasp when I realize what he's doing. His eyes flick up to mine. "You ready, Goddess?"

"For what?" I pant, fighting the urge to roll my hips.

He smirks, his brow cocking. "For that," he chuckles. "To fuck my fist." I moan, tipping my head back as I give into the desire to rock my hips. "That a girl. Ride me hard, and don't stop until this greedy pussy is gushing all over me. I want to be covered in you, Tinsley. Fucking drenched. You got me?"

I shudder but nod, not understanding his words. I hear the quiet *beep* of the record button on his phone and do my best to ignore it as I lift up and down. All five of his fingers are inside of me, but I don't think I've taken him all yet. I don't even think I can. But it doesn't stop the orgasm I can feel barreling into me at just the knowledge that I've done this much. Taken this much of him.

"This is the hottest thing I've ever seen," he breathes. "I'm gonna nut in my fucking pants here, Tinsley. *Jesus.*"

I smile, relishing his words. My hands slide up my naked skin, over my belly, and up to my chest. I look back down, locking eyes with Nico as I grope my breasts and pinch my nipples. I feel the small droplets sliding down my fingers and do something I know will set him off. I lift them to my mouth and lick my fingers clean with a moan.

He groans, and the phone clatters to the floor beside us. "Fuck," he grunts. All at once, his thumb finds my clit, and his fist fucks up inside of me. Though it's rough, it's not deep, and he's careful not to hurt me. He somehow curves his hand and brushes my g-spot while vigorously rubbing my clit.

"Cum for me, Tinsley. Fucking cum right now. Show me what a good girl you can be for Daddy." I shake my head. It's too much. Too much. "Just breathe, baby. You have to relax."

The burning sensation inside of me breaks like a damn as I do as I'm told. Head thrown back, nails digging into his hard chest, I scream out my release. Liquid pours from me, coating my thighs and his stomach in a never-ending release. It goes on and on until I feel faint and light-headed.

Panting, I look down, finding his eyes closed and his chest heaving. His very wet chest. Gaping, I try to scramble back, but he's still inside of me. "Nico," I screech. "Did my water just break?"

His eyes snap open, and his lip curls up in a smile. He shakes his head and gently removes his hand from my throbbing pussy. More liquid escapes, and I really start to panic. He rubs his opposite hand up and down my thigh calmly. "No, Goddess. You squirted, and it was fucking incredible."

"You're soaked," I state. "I'm—"

"Don't you dare apologize, Tinsley." He sucks his hand clean, licking up every inch of my mess he can reach. "Delicious."

Swallowing, I look down, finding a wet patch over his jeans. "Did you?" I whisper.

Chuckling, he shakes his head. "No. That's all you. I almost did, but I was too lost in watching you to even think about myself."

Reaching for his zipper, I free him, ignoring him when he tells me it's fine. It's not. And it's not always about me. His cock is ridged, pulsing, and an angry shade of red as it slaps against his wet stomach. The sound is obscene, and it makes both of us groan. My fists wrap around him, unsurprised when my fingers don't meet.

His body jolts beneath me, and he squeezes my thighs. "I'm so close," he chokes out. "So fucking close just from watching you."

"I want—" I breathe, stroking him up and down. I forget my words as I become entranced by the sight of Nico falling apart under my hands. I pay attention to his cues and his body language to determine what he does and doesn't like. What brings him closer to the edge. It's intoxicating.

His nails bite into my flesh as his breathing picks up. "What do you want, baby?" he whispers, his eyes hooded. "Say it."

"I want you to cum inside me," I murmur, swirling my thumb around the sticky strings of precum leaking from his thick tip. Flicking my eyes up, I lick my lips. "Please?"

"Put me in you," he demands, his voice guttural. "Right fucking now."

Leaning up, I press him to my entrance and slide down, fully sheathing him easily. He may have just stretched me wide, but the feeling of Nico's hard cock inside my pussy feels different. Hot. Pulsing. *Deep.*

"Yes," he groans, gripping my hips. He lifts me up, using me to fuck himself as though I'm his own personal toy to use while uttering jumbled words. "Squeezing me so hard. So wet. Fucking perfect. Mine. Mine. *Mine.*"

Nico cums with a roar, shoving me down hard and forcing me to take every drop of his cum. His body trembles as I clench around him, keeping him exactly where he is. We're both panting as he comes down from his release. We're sweaty and sticky, covered in all sorts of fluids. But we're wearing matching smiles, and I find that I don't really give a shit how I look. I feel amazing. Freer than I've ever been before and...sexy. Really fucking sexy.

He brushes damn hair from my face, tucking it behind my ear. "I love you, Goddess."

Smiling, I press a kiss on his wrist. "I love you too, Mr. Saint."

# Chapter Seventeen

## nicolai saint

"Thank you all for coming here today," I greet, nodding at the 32 board members gathered in the Wonderland conference room. I look to Kevin last, tilting my lip up in a secretive smile. He's the only one that knows why we're here today. After months of arguing and deliberation, I've decided to take the decision out of their hands. "I appreciate you all joining us on such short notice, especially since it's the week before Christmas."

"Why are we here, Nicolai?" Charlie Johnson quips, leaning back in his chair. The leather creaks beneath his weight, and I barely hold in an eye roll. Men like Charlie are why I won't be sad to walk away from this.

Kevin beats me to it. "Have somewhere better to be, Charles?" He drums his fingers on the glass tabletop, a mischievous glint in his eyes. "Your wife's sister's house, perhaps?" A round of snickers follows Kev's words. I grin.

Charlie's cheeks immediately turn red. His fists clench and unclench repeatedly. He rolls his neck and smirks before turning his lethal glare on me. "Don't *you* have somewhere better to be, Nico?" He shrugs, and I already know I'll want to kill him for his next words. "Like your little girlfriend's barely legal cu—"

"I wouldn't finish that sentence if I were you, Charles," a cold feminine voice snaps. I let out a shaky breath instead of the growl in my chest but can't bring myself to look away from the prick who will probably be fired by this evening. "I know Cherish and her sister Kate very well. I have no problem picking up the phone right now and letting them both know what a piece of cheating, manipulative shit you are."

I smile, dropping down into my chair. Yeah. I'm definitely doing the right thing. I finally turn toward the newcomer and toss her a wink.

"Welcome, Candance," I greet, gesturing to the open seat next to me. At the head of the table.

She shifts awkwardly, her eyes wide and confused. I tilt my head again and arch a brow, daring her to deny wanting this. She squeezes her hands together tightly and forces her back straight before gliding across the large room. Candy lets out a long breath and gently takes her seat. I glance around the room, wanting to see everyone's reactions. As I assumed, everyone but one person is either smiling or misty-eyed. A few of the women who have been with Wonderland the longest are even crying.

"Everyone. I'd like you to meet the new CEO of the Wonderland Corporation." I flick my glaze to Candy's. "If she accepts, that is."

I swear, if I didn't know she hates guns, I'd say Candy's about to shoot me. She rolls her shoulders back, batting away errant tears, and nods before looking at her new board. "I'd be honored."

The room falls into a fit of happy cheers and congratulations. I give them a few minutes before gesturing for them to take their seats and settle down. I stand and clear my throat, looking at one of my oldest friends. My surrogate grandmother. My family.

"Candance," I start, smiling. "I can't explain how much it's meant to me to have you not only as a part of the Wonderland family but my own. You love this company as though it's your baby. You take care of it. You love it. You look out for it." I shake my head. "I don't know where I'd be without you, but I do know that Wonderland wouldn't be the same."

"Shit," she murmurs, wiping away her tears and making the rest of us chuckle.

I clap once, giving a final nod. "Alright. So, with all that aside, please enjoy the Christmas feast our wonderful catering team has set up for you in conference room three and welcome Candance to Wonderland Co."

Everyone expresses their warm wishes, shaking Candy's hand or hugging her. I stand back, happy to watch my friend get the congratulatory praise she deserves. Everything in the last month and a half has been a whirlwind. But through it all, Candy has stayed by my side, just like she has for the last ten years. She really does deserve this and so much more.

I'm about to tell her that when my phone vibrates in my pocket. My eyes flick to the clock on the far wall, and my brows dip. I slide it from my slacks, finding a number that has my heart dropping flashing across the screen. I accept, pressing the phone to my ear, my feet already moving to the door. I shoot a panicked wave at Candy. She gives me a soft look and a thumbs up, looking more choked up now than she was before.

"Lottie? What's wrong? Where's Tinsley?" My girl was supposed to be putting finishing touches on the nursery with Lottie this morning since she's due in a week.

Lottie sucks in a breath, and I bolt for the elevator, my heart lodged in my throat. "She's in the hospital. The baby's coming, Nico. Hurry your ass up."

*Fuck.*

Luckily, Gresham General is only a thirty-minute drive from the Wonderland building, but I still make it to the hospital by the skin of my teeth. My feet pound up three flights of stairs, not having the time to fuck around with the long elevator line. I burst into the delivery wing, my body covered in a thin sheen of sweat, my heart pounding so hard, I might need to visit the ER after this.

"Where is she?" I bark at the first nurse I see. I swallow, remembering she needs more words than that. "Tinsley Snow. Or Saint. I don't know what she'd put." If my girl decided to come in here claiming she's a Saint, I'd have no choice but to call an officiant and make her one.

The woman stutters briefly but takes in the likely murderous look on my face and nods before checking a tablet in her hands. She swallows. "Uh," pointing down the long hall, she grimaces. "Room 231 on the left. But, sir, you better hurry. Says she's ready to push."

That's all I need to know. Emotions I've never felt before ricochet through every inch of my being. My nerve endings are repeatedly misfiring, making me feel alive and seconds from passing out simultaneously. Adrenaline, anxiety, and fear mix with joy, love, and gratitude, creating a heady concoction.

I skid to a stop outside her door, taking a second to get my shit together. I need to be strong for Tinsley. I need to be her rock right now. I can't fall apart. Swallowing, I squeeze my eyes shut and shake out my hands. That's when I hear it. A blood-curdling scream.

I shove through the door, not even bothering with knocking. I vaguely notice two or three people in scrubs out of the corner of my eye, but nothing, *nothing*, would be able to pull my attention from the woman sprawled out on the bed before me.

Long pale-blonde hair fanned out over a white pillow. Red, sweaty cheeks. Ice blue eyes. Thick red lips. A tear-stained face. And love. So much fucking love.

Love she makes known as she sighs happily with an exhausted smile. "*Nico.*"

"Goddess," I breathe. It hits me then. Slams into me with a force so strong, I almost buckle to my knees.

I'm about to be a father.

We may be new, but there is no doubt in my mind that the woman in front of me is mine. Mine for the rest of my days, no matter how long or short they may be. She's my love. My wife. My future. The mother of my children. My whole goddamned world.

And... we're going to be parents.

Any second if the scream that rips from her throat is any indication. I shake away my wild emotions and chaotic thoughts and close the distance between us. I waste no time wrapping my arm behind her neck, supporting her while she pushes. Tinsley releases a shuddering breath at the contact.

"I'm here, baby. You're doing so good. So good. I'm so fucking proud of you." I whisper words of encouragement just for her. I cover her sweat-damp hair in kisses. When she reaches for my hand, I let her squeeze it as hard as she needs. This woman could break all of my fingers. Shatter them altogether—and I'd smile, reminding her how well she's doing.

Less than thirty minutes later, we welcome our first daughter, Noelle Pixie Saint, into this world. She's tiny like her mom, with a head full of white-blond hair, something that Tinsley sobs over. I have my guesses as to why, but I keep my mouth shut. That bastard has no place in this room or in our lives. Not today. Not ever.

The nurse swaddles Noelle in a candy cane striped blanket and passes her to Tinsley. Sitting on the bed next to her, with my girls in my arms, I feel more complete than I have in my entire life.

Almost.

I press my lips to Tinsley's temple, the back of my finger swiping across Noelle's soft, pink cheek, and inhale their scents. My eyes burn, and I let the tears come. They wouldn't be the first. I cried throughout the entire delivery. Probably more than Tinsley did.

"I love you, Goddess." Tinsley sniffles, turning her face to meet mine. She offers me her mouth, which I greedily take. My palm cups the back of the baby's head, keeping her safely tucked into her mama's chest while we're distracted. The kiss is full of all the things I can't possibly put into words, no matter how many times I might try. I pour every unspoken vow, every emotion, and declaration into her, not pulling away until we're breathless. Pressing my lips to her ear, I murmur the only thing that can't be said with a kiss alone. "Marry me."

Tinsley sucks in a sharp breath and nods against my cheek. "Yes, please, Mr. Saint."

I let out a raspy chuckle and cuff the back of her neck, bringing her mouth to mine. Before our lips connect, I murmur, "Christmas fucking miracle, indeed."

# Epilogue

## One Year Later

## TINSLEY SNOW

"Bad, Stella," I cry, running toward the tree just as the psychopath barrels her way up to the top. I screech when the whole thing wobbles precariously to the left. "No. Bad. Very, very bad."

She stares down and me, and if I didn't know any better, I'd say she's smiling. In slow motion, she darts out one tiny white paw and lifts it toward an ornament.

"Don't you dare," I hiss, regretting the decision to go for a 12-foot Christmas tree when I'm the size of an actual elf. She makes a chuffing sound and darts her tiny foot out, batting the ornament hard enough to send it skittering to the floor. It bounces once, twice, before rolling under the coffee table. I sigh and shoot her a cocky look. "Not what you were expecting, huh?" I lift my shoulders. "What did you expect? We can't exactly have breakable things in a house this wild, can we?"

This time, I *know* she's laughing at me because seconds later, the telltale sound of a pack of wild animals galloping through the house fills the air. I groan, dropping my head in defeat. Another ornament hits the ground, and then another. They barely hit the ground before being snatched up by said wild animals. Vixen and Prancer are the first to run away with my soft, fuzzy reindeer that I specially chose for our tree, knowing Pixie would be all over them like white on rice. I swear, having a house filled with eight dogs, one demonic cat, and a one-year-old is insanity. Happy, beautiful, rewarding, and never dull, but insane, nonetheless.

"You guys are trying to give mommy a migraine, aren't you?" I groan as Comet, Donner, and Blitzen spot Stella hanging out at the top of the tree and lose their ever-loving shit. "Where is your father when I need him?"

"What in the world is going on in here?" Nico shouts, his voice just south of frantic. "Is everything okay?"

I groan, dropping my ass on the couch and resting my head back. Thank God. Not my monkeys, not my circus. Well, that's not true. They're all mine. But not today. Today was supposed to be my *me* day to finish wrapping gifts and preparing for Christmas while Nico's at work. But it's just been one thing after another. I haven't even had time to clean or shower or...Christ. When's the last time I ate?

I sigh. Mom life.

"Goddess?" Nico murmurs, dropping down next to me. I blink my eyes open, noticing that the chaos is gone, and Stella is no longer trying to take my tree down, one ornament at a time.

"Where'd they go?" I ask, arching a brow.

He chuckles, tucking my much shorter hair behind my ear. A few months ago, I decided having hair down to my ass wasn't great, considering Pixie is now starting to walk and loves to tug and chew on everything. And let me tell you, that girl may be tiny like me, but she has a grip like her fathers, or so Nico likes to say. Dirty man.

"I put them outside. Penn will be here any minute to take them to the park." I exhale, leaning my head against his shoulder. "What's wrong, baby? Are you okay?"

"I'm just exhausted," I murmur. "There's so much to take care of around here and with the foundation." Both Nico and I run the Saint Foundation full-time now. It's one of the most gratifying things I have ever had the privilege of being a part of. But it's tiring. "Plus, I haven't been sleeping well."

He chuckles, squeezing my thigh. "If I remember correctly, you're the one that kept me up last night."

I scoff but don't deny it. What can I say? A year later, I still can't get enough of my husband. From the very first day I met him, things have been like this. We're insatiable for each other. We may have twenty-five years between us, but those years feel like nothing. He was meant for me, and I him. Nico completes me. Not only that, but he's the best father in the world to Pixie. Sometimes I think she loves him more than she loves me. They have a bond that I didn't think was possible. Especially not with how she got her start in life. But it's a bond I'm grateful for every single day.

"Really, though." He tilts my chin up, his brows furrowed in concern. "You look exhausted. Is something on your mind?"

The glimmer in his eye and the tiny line next to his lips where I can't tell he's fighting a smirk gives me pause. Does he know? No. He can't possibly know. I only just found out last week. I narrow my eyes at him and shake my head.

"I just really want to take a shower and wash my hair." Sitting up, I yawn loudly. "Better yet. Maybe I'll take a bath."

Nico rubs my back, nodding. "Sounds like a good idea. Why don't I pour you a glass of wine, and you can go relax."

I push off the couch, stretch my arms over my head, and groan. "I can't have win—"

*Fuck.*

He clears his throat, sliding his hands into his pockets. I turn my wide eyes onto his, finding him smirking with his head cocked to the side.

"What's that, now, Goddess?" he mutters, his voice thick with heat as his eyes rake down my body, zeroing in on my flat belly.

I swallow. Well, Jingle Balls.

Unable to hold the secret in any longer, I rush to the Christmas tree and pull out the tiny box I stashed there a few days ago. I slide back across the wooden floor in my knee-high socks, grinning like a loon and bouncing in place.

"Merry Christmas, Mr. Saint," I breathe, handing him the package. It's simple, non-descript, and full of the biggest secret I've ever kept. Well, from him, that is. Nico and I don't keep secrets. It's impossible when you're glued to each other's sides the way we are.

Nico releases a shuddering breath, clutching the box hard. His eyes are already misty because we both know what's inside this box.

After Pixie was born, we talked seriously about having more children. From the first moment I saw Nico with her, I knew I wanted more. I knew I'd want a whole house full of Nico's babies. He agreed. But, despite how easily I conceived the first go around, that wasn't the case this time. For a while, Nico worried it was him. So much so that he went and had his sperm checked. He was terrified that due to his age, he wouldn't be able to give us any more children himself. Luckily, he was totally fine, and Dr. Talbot insisted that some things just take time. Sure enough...time was all we needed.

That, and some really filthy sex.

"Goddess," he swallows, untying the ribbon. It flutters to the ground, quickly followed by the lid and tissue paper. Tears fill my eyes as I watch Nico lift the ornament Pixie and I made for him last week. "Holy fucking shit," he chokes out. "Are you sure?"

I nod, pressing my hand to my belly. "8 weeks today."

The ornament is a green circle with Pixie's tiny handprint in the middle in white. The words "Best Daddy Ever" are in red on the top, and on the bottom, it says, "Times Two."

He stares at it in awe for countless minutes before shaking his head and charging forward. He bundles me up in his arms, spinning me around in circles. I wrap my arms and legs around him, holding him tightly while we cry and celebrate this gift...this miracle.

"I love you so fucking much, Tinsley." I bury my face in his neck, inhaling his juniper, balsam, and cinnamon scent. Christmas. Nico. *Mine*. "Thank you, baby. Thank you. Thank you. Thank you."

I chuckle, shaking my head. "Thank *you*, Nicolai. I don't know where I'd be without you."

*This* is exactly how it should have been before. Finding out I was pregnant with Pixie while sobbing in a public restroom at a bus stop, alone and terrified, was the lowest point in my life. I had no idea that just two years later, things would turn out so utterly perfect. With my arms wrapped around the best man I've ever known, the love of my life, and the life we created between us. Nothing could make this moment better.

A crackling sound breaks through our tears, freezing us both in place. "Mamamama. Dada-dada." The babbled words coming over the baby monitor have me sobbing even harder.

*Now*, this moment can't get any better.

# Want More

## From The Blue River Crew?

Guess whose book is next...
I'll give you a hint. You first met them in Primal Urges. It's the bitchiest of bitches that you'll hate to love but love so much, and the only man ever to put her in her place.
You guessed it...*or not.*
Jack and Addy are coming to you in a filthy Valentine's Day one-night stand.
Or is it?
Only time will tell.
Keep your eyes peeled for more information about their Valentine's Novella,
***Power Struggle***

# Also By

## Author Bex Dawn

The Los Diablos world encompasses these three series (for now!)
For full reading order, please visit my website.
They are all still growing, but these are the books you can read/preorder now!

### Los Diablos Syndicate
Crash(Prequel)
Burn
Evolve
Resurrect
Prevail

### The Trichotomy of New York
Violet Craves (Prequel)
Rough Love
Tough Love

## Sons Of Satan MC
Brass: Part One
Chains

This series is a separate world. These are stand-alone, loosely interwoven, that take place in the town of Blue River, Colorado.
They each follow a different couple, and their very specific kinks!

## Carnal Expectations
Cracked Foundation
Primal Urges
Santa's Baby
Power Struggle

# About Author

## Bex Dawn

*H**I, THERE SMUTTY BUDDY!*
*Welcome to my world.*
*I'm a 30-something bibliophile from California. I own a beauty salon, five rescue animals, and a shit ton of books. I have been writing since I could hold a pencil. My mom used to love to tell stories about the "books" I would write as a child. I would apparently scribble nonsense on paper and then proceed to "read" my books to everyone who would listen. Not much has changed since other than the fact that I've changed out the pencil and paper for a fancy laptop.*

*Writing and creative arts have always held a place close to my heart, but it wasn't until an extremely dark time in my life recently, that I really pushed myself to fulfill my lifelong dream of publishing.*

*In the darkest days of my life, books saved me. Other people's written words dragged me out of my depression, kicking and screaming. And for that, I will forever be grateful. My dream is that my words will have a similar impact on even one person out there.*

*So, here's to sexy, possessive, alpha holes and kinky fuckery!*

Follow me on social media!

www.authorbexdawn.com

TikTok: @bexdawnwrites

Instagram: @bexdawnwrites

Amazon: Bex Dawn

Facebook
: Author Bex Dawn

Linktree for all other links and points of contact!

Printed in Great Britain
by Amazon